'I don't recall inviting you in.'

Her voice was cold. 'You might like to leave before I call the police.'

A sensible man wway, but Nick had n   lly was concerned.

'Sal, talk to   What's wrong?'

'Nothing's wrong, except that you're standing in my hallway and I want you to leave.'

'Don't change the subject. You know what I mean. What happened all those years ago that made you ring me?'

For an age she hesitated, as if she was engaged in some internal struggle, then the fight seemed to go out of her.

'I had a baby,' she said, so quietly that for a moment he wondered if he'd heard right.

Then the impact of her words hit home, and he stared at her in shock. 'A baby?' he echoed. He sucked in some much-needed air. 'You mean I'm a father? All these years I've been a father and I didn't even know?'

Caroline Anderson has the mind of a butterfly. She's been a nurse, a secretary, a teacher, has run her own soft-furnishing business and now she's settled on writing. She says, 'I was looking for that elusive something. I finally realised it was variety, and now I have it in abundance. Every book brings new horizons and new friends, and in between books I have learned to be a juggler. My teacher husband John and I have two beautiful daughters, Sarah and Hannah, umpteen pets and several acres of Suffolk that nature tries to reclaim every time we turn our backs!' Caroline also writes for the Tender Romance™ series.

Recent titles by the same author:

RESCUING DR RYAN
A MOTHER BY NATURE
GIVE ME FOREVER
JUST A FAMILY DOCTOR

ACCIDENTAL RENDEZVOUS

BY
CAROLINE ANDERSON

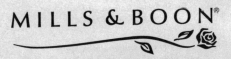

All the characters in this book have no existence outside the imagination
of the author, and have no relation whatsoever to anyone bearing the
same name or names. They are not even distantly inspired by any
individual known or unknown to the author, and all the incidents are
pure invention.

First published in Great Britain 2001
Harlequin Mills & Boon Limited,
Eton House, 18-24 Paradise Road, Richmond, Surrey TW9 1SR

© Caroline Anderson 2001

ISBN 0 263 82685 6

Set in Times Roman 10½ on 12 pt.
03-0901-44546

Printed and bound in Spain
by Litografía Rosés, S.A., Barcelona

CHAPTER ONE

SHE would have known that laugh anywhere.

It rippled down the corridor, bringing smiles to the faces of the people who heard it, raising a chuckle here and there, leaving no one untouched. It was a rich, warm laugh; a deep laugh, spontaneous and generous, the laugh of a man who knew how to enjoy life.

It nearly brought Sally to her knees.

Heart pounding, her mouth dry, the strength in her legs vanishing by the second, she propped herself up against the nearest wall and sucked in a slow, steadying breath.

Not Nick. Please, God, not Nick. Not here, not now. Not ever! Seven years hadn't made it any easier to think about him, and if she imagined she'd got over him, well, now she knew that lie for what it was.

She could hear footsteps approaching, and the low murmur of masculine voices, and before she could prise herself from the wall and run for cover Ryan O'Connor, the senior A and E consultant, appeared around the corner with another man at his side—a man that Sally had longed for and yet had hoped never to see again—and she was trapped.

'Ah, Sally! Just the person I was looking for,' Ryan said with a broad smile. 'Meet Dr Nick Baker, my new specialist registrar.'

Reluctantly, her throat working convulsively to

swallow the huge lump that had appeared as if by magic, she let her eyes move from Ryan to Nick.

How odd, she thought with the small, distant part of her brain that still seemed to be functioning. He's changed, and yet he's exactly the same.

Her eyes, greedy for him, took inventory. Solidly built, a shade under six feet, his mid-brown hair shorter than it used to be but still rumpled and untidy, his eyes the same astonishing blue behind the character lines that bracketed them now, his mouth mobile and expressive, the smile every bit as sexy as it had ever been—

'Hello, Sally,' he murmured, and the voice like dark chocolate slithered over her nerve endings and brought her hormones snapping to attention.

'Hello, Nick,' she said automatically, and then Ryan's words sank in. *New specialist registrar*? she thought frantically. He's *working* here? Belatedly she noticed the white coat, the stethoscope slung casually round his neck, the name badge on his pocket.

Thank goodness she was still propped up against the wall, because at that moment, without it, she would have fallen over with the shock.

'Sally's a tyrant,' Ryan was saying with a hint of laughter in his soft Canadian voice. 'Stay on the right side of her and you'll be OK, but she runs a tight ship and she doesn't suffer fools gladly. Her temper's legendary.'

'That hasn't changed, then,' Nick murmured, his eyes scanning her, and she felt the touch of his gaze like fingers of fire over her body.

'Hey, Sally, your reputation seems to have preceded you,' Ryan said with an amused chuckle, but Nick shook his head, his eyes never leaving her.

'No. We're old buddies—aren't we, Sal?' he replied, and his eyes challenged her to defy him.

'Absolutely,' she said, still groping for a coherent thought. She dredged up a smile, hopefully not too inane, and switched her gaze pointedly to Ryan. 'Well, to be exact, we *were* old buddies. We worked together, many years ago—'

'Seven,' Nick said softly.

And she thought, He remembers. How odd. I'm surprised he can even be bothered to remember my name. She cranked up the smile.

'Is it really? Good heavens.'

A strong brow twitched sceptically, but he let it go, his mouth tipping in an answering smile more genuine than her own. 'It's good to see you again.'

He was holding out his hand, and without a huge breach of social etiquette it would have been impossible to ignore it. Heart pounding, she placed her hand in his and felt the shock of that contact, the first in seven years, to the tips of her toes.

His hand was hard and warm and dry, his fingers curling round hers. His thumb brushed against the outside of her wrist—by accident? It sent quivers of reaction up the nerves in her arm.

She snatched her hand back as soon as was decently possible, but not before the impact of that everyday social gesture had played havoc with her blood pressure and turned her already weakened legs to jelly.

Ryan grinned at her. 'Well, since you two know each other, why don't I leave you to show Nick round the department and catch up on old times? I have a couple of letters to dictate and some calls to make while we're quiet.'

'Quiet? You do know how to tempt fate, don't you?' she said with what she hoped was her usual cynicism, struggling for a normal tone that didn't betray her shock. Not for the world did she want Nick to know he still had any effect on her—and especially not *that* effect! She turned to him as Ryan walked away.

'I don't have long,' she said crisply. 'I'm briefing some new nurses in a few minutes, but I can give you a quick whizz round and show you the basics. The rest you'll pick up as you go along.'

'I'm sure you'll put me straight if I don't,' he murmured, his voice tinged with irony, and she had a flicker of guilt. It was stupid to fall out with him over nothing. Whatever lay behind them, they still had to work together in the near future, and there was no point in them getting off on the wrong foot. And Ryan's remark about her temper hadn't helped at all.

'I'm not really the dragon he made me out to be,' she told him, embarrassed by Ryan's summing up of her character.

'I'm sure you're not,' he said mildly.

She sneaked a sideways glance at him, but his face was bland and innocent of any expression. Huh! He always had been a hell of a poker player. She wondered if he'd known she was here. He hadn't seemed surprised to see her—or maybe she just didn't have the effect on him that he had on her. Even so, after all this time and after what they'd been to each other, she would have expected *some* reaction.

She took him round the department, introducing him to people, showing him the layout, while her mind whirled.

Coincidence, or not? Most people tended to stick to one particular part of the country for their specialist training, because it made for a less disrupted social life. It wasn't always possible, of course, and sometimes people were forced to move away for a rotation.

The last time she'd known his whereabouts, he'd been in Manchester, well away from Suffolk, so maybe disruption wasn't something that worried him, or maybe he'd moved on long ago.

Whatever, even if he'd been training within their region for some time, that covered umpteen hospitals scattered all across East Anglia. However, only so many had an A and E department of any size or note, so it was almost inevitable they'd end up together at some point. He would hardly have to engineer it. It could quite easily have been coincidence.

What she didn't know, of course, and couldn't find out—short of asking him, which was totally out of the question—was whether he *had* deliberately chosen a rotation here at the Audley Memorial, or if it was an accident of fate. Absolutely the last thing she intended to do was sound even slightly interested in his personal life or his reason for doing anything— but she would like to know...

Anyway, in her heart she knew the answer. After their acrimonious and bitter parting, and most especially after he'd failed to answer her plea when she'd needed him—really, *really* needed him—there was no way that he'd have come looking for her.

Which left coincidence.

All she had to decide now was whether she could survive it.

'Sally, RTA coming in, several casualties, more to follow,' her young staff nurse, Meg, said as she hurried up to them. 'I've warned the front desk and they're clearing Resus.'

'Thanks. You might dig Ryan out of his office—he's trying to do paperwork. He'll probably welcome you with open arms. And put those new girls with someone doing something routine, could you? I don't want to frighten them both off on their first morning.' Nick, on the other hand, was a different proposition altogether. She turned to him and gave him a grim smile. 'OK, then. Let's see how the boy wonder shaped up, shall we?'

His answering smile was equally grim. 'Why do I get the feeling I'm on trial here?' he murmured, and, dropping a casual hand on her shoulder, he turned her round and headed back towards Resus.

She could hear sirens in the distance, and she hurried to prepare everything in readiness for the influx. Patients were shuffled, reassured and soothed, equipment was checked, Ambulance Control quizzed again as to the exact number and severity of their casualties.

Through it all she could feel the imprint of his palm—could still feel it, hours later, when all the blood and mayhem had subsided and they were back to the usual level of pandemonium that passed for normality in the department.

Well, Nick thought, as introductions to a job went, this one couldn't have been much tougher. They'd been working side by side, and if he hadn't known better he would have thought Sally had been keeping an eye on him.

Checking him out, no less, making sure he was up to speed.

Damn cheek! His mouth tipped into the faintest grin. It had its upside, though. He'd spent the morning hip to hip and shoulder to shoulder with her, locked together in the battle to save their patients.

He hadn't had time to think about what he'd been doing and whether she'd approve of it. He'd just gone into autopilot, working flat out to save first one, then another of the casualties. He'd had to rely on her, and she'd been there, keeping pace with him every step of the way.

She'd been amazing to work with—fast, efficient, precise—a real treasure. She would have been a brilliant doctor, and she was plenty clever enough, but as she'd told him all those years ago, it wasn't what she wanted to do.

She wanted to nurse, and she was still doing it, although she was far enough up the ladder now to be in a nurse manager's post, instead of remaining on the shop floor so to speak, in amongst it.

It was where she belonged, of course, working in a highly skilled and specialised post where her undoubted talents were exploited to the full.

And they have been today, heaven knows, Nick thought. He pictured again the frightened young mother they'd had to stabilise, and Sally's gentle reassurance as he'd explored the full extent of her injuries. She'd kept the woman calm, focused her mind on the positive and all the time she'd been working beside him, assisting him and keeping him updated with the woman's status.

And now it was lunchtime, his stomach told him, and if there was a God at all he'd get a few minutes off and time to talk Sally into a cup of coffee and a sandwich. After all, as Ryan had said, they had a lot of catching up to do.

There was no God, of course, or if there was He was having lunch Himself. There was nothing drastic, just a steady stream of casualties ranging from the life-threatened to the frankly malingering, and it was ages before he saw her again.

She accosted him as he went from the work station back towards a cubicle with an X-ray result.

'Have you had a break recently?' she said almost accusingly.

He shook his head, wondering if that was an unpardonable sin in her strictly run department or if she was about to proposition him. 'No, I haven't had time.'

'Nor have I,' she confessed. 'Grab a moment and come into the staffroom when you've dealt with that—is it straightforward?'

A proposition? Maybe there was a God after all. He nodded again. 'Yes—a query fracture that isn't. It just needs Tubigrip and advice.'

'Right. I'll make you a coffee and guard the biscuits if there are any. I don't want you keeling over. Be quick.'

He changed his mind. It sounded like the unpardonable sin option, to his disappointment. Ah, well.

He was quick—as quick as he could be without neglecting the patient's interests—and then, reminding himself that he wasn't the only doctor on duty and he needed a break if he was to be of any real use for the rest of his shift, he walked determinedly past a crying child in the next cubicle, past a nurse carrying a set of notes who tried to hail him, and into the staffroom.

Sally was in there with her back to him, bending over to retrieve something from a cupboard, and he was treated to the curve of her bottom and a peep of slender legs when her skirt rode up as she turned towards him.

'The coffee's run out,' she said in disgust. 'Will tea do?'

'Tea's fine,' he assured her, wondering if he was going to make a public disgrace of himself and dragging his eyes from the long sweep of her thigh. She straightened, to his simultaneous relief and disappointment, and started clattering mugs about.

'So, how are things going?' she asked over her shoulder.

He went closer, just to be near her, to stand within range of the scent of her skin and feel the warmth from her body.

Not that he was cold—far from it. 'Things are going fine,' he murmured, and she jumped and whirled round.

'Do you have to creep up on me?' she said crossly, and to his delight she looked flustered—flustered and every bit as beautiful as she ever had. He smiled.

'Sorry—just coming to get my mug from you,' he said innocently.

She made a noise under her breath that could have been anything but was probably disgust, and stuck a mug in his hand. 'White, no sugar, not too much milk—that right still?'

She remembers, he thought, and felt a stab of regret. 'Yes, that's right still,' he said softly. Grabbing a handful of biscuits from the tin she offered him, he retreated to the other side of the room, dropped into a comfy chair and crossed one ankle over the other knee to give his feelings a little privacy.

He'd been too busy earlier to react, but now, with this little homely act, she'd brought back a whole host of memories he really didn't have the time to deal with.

'So how've you been?' he asked in what he hoped was a level voice, and she shrugged and smiled brightly. Too brightly.

'Oh, fine. Busy. You?'

He shrugged. 'So-so. Busy, like you. Too busy, really.'

'Is that why you're here, in the country, looking for a change of pace?' she asked, a touch of disapproval in her voice. 'If so, I hate to disappoint you but we run flat out all day and all night. Even country bumpkins have accidents.'

He gave a soft, wry laugh. 'Is that what you think? That I'm looking for a quiet life? I haven't altered that much.'

Her eyes scanned him almost guiltily, and she looked away. 'No, I don't suppose you have,' she said, and her voice sounded gruff and a little taut.

'Anyway,' he said, just to make the point, 'I've been working in country hospitals for years now, so it's hardly a change of pace.'

'No.' She stood up, put a little cold water in her

tea from the tap and drained it, then all but dropped the mug on the worktop in her haste. 'I have to get on. I'll see you later.'

'What are you doing after work?' he asked impulsively, stopping her in her tracks.

Slowly, as if she was giving herself time, she turned towards him. 'Nothing,' she said clearly. 'Either with you, or anyone else.'

And she turned on her heel and walked away.

He gave a slow smile. It was a putdown, without a shadow of a doubt, but it had failed. 'Either with you, or anyone else,' she'd said, and that left the smile on his face, because if there was one thing he didn't want to do, it was tread on someone else's toes and upset things for her if she'd got her life on track.

And if she wasn't doing anything with anyone else, then from where he was sitting right now that was a definite plus.

But progress, he thought with a laughing sigh, was clearly going to be measured in microns...

'Why, oh, why, oh why—?'

'Sally?'

She looked up at Ryan, standing beside her and eyeing her quizzically. 'Hi, there,' she said brightly. 'Problem?'

'Not me,' he said, his eyes all too perceptive. 'It was you I was worried about. Are you OK?'

'Me? Of course,' she lied.

'Just wondered. You looked a little poleaxed earlier. It just occurred to me that you and Nick might have had something going once. I hope it won't be a problem.'

'No problem,' she assured him with false cheer, and wondered if it could possibly be true or if it was going to be, as she suspected, a living nightmare until he moved on again. Perhaps it was time to take some in-service training—in Alaska or somewhere. Maybe Ryan could recommend a nice, remote Canadian hospital—

'Just wondering, that's all,' Ryan murmured. 'You want to talk to me, you know where to find me.'

'Ryan, thanks, but I'm fine. It was over years ago, and it was nothing much anyway,' she assured him, and wondered why God didn't strike her down for such a whopper.

Or maybe it was the truth, and it really had been nothing much, only she'd been too lovestruck and besotted to realise it.

With a sharp sigh, she snatched up the next set of notes, shot through the cubicles and went out to the heaving waiting room. With any luck she'd be able to avoid him for the rest of the day. She scanned the crowd.

'Mrs Johnson? Can you come through, please?'

Luck wasn't on her side that day. A scant hour later, Sally stuck her head round the corner of the cubicle where Nick was working and beckoned him.

'Could I have a quick word, Dr Baker?' she murmured.

'Sure. Excuse me a moment.'

He stood up and ducked through the curtain, raising a brow quizzically. 'Problem?'

'I will have. There's an attempted suicide coming in,' she told him quietly. 'Young woman who's thrown herself out of a third-floor window—facial and pelvic injuries. Ryan's gone to a meeting, Matt's on holiday and the new SHO is so wet behind the ears I daren't trust him with a Band-Aid.'

He grinned, sending her off kilter again, and nodded. 'I'll get this one sorted out and come through to Resus. Five minutes?'

'Maximum.'

'OK. Get the mobile X-ray in there with a radiographer, and call an anaesthetist in case we have airway problems.'

'Done it.'

'Good girl.' With a wink, he ducked back behind the curtain, and she ignored her skittering heart and went into Resus to make sure it was ready for the new arrival.

It was back to normal after the mayhem of the morning, thanks to the cleaners and the nurses who'd restocked the supplies. Thinking of the facial injuries and the effect they might have on the patient's airway, she checked their stock of all the different sorts of airway the anaesthetist might need, and then went out to meet the ambulance, just as Nick emerged from his cubicle and headed towards the door.

'Perfect timing,' she said as the ambulance backed up and the doors opened. As the trolley was lifted out, she winced inwardly. Their casualty was a mess—she was on a spinal board, her face was trashed and her colour was lousy despite the oxygen mask held lightly in place.

The paramedic gave them a quick rundown as they wheeled her rapidly into Resus.

'Twenty-five-year-old female, name of Jodie

Farmer, neighbour saw her jump off her third-floor balcony. She landed on the concrete path outside. GCS 15 at the scene. She needs a tube down really but I thought I'd leave that to you guys as she's still able to breathe and we were only round the corner— watch her jaw, it's shattered and her tongue's bleeding. She'd got umpteen teeth missing, too. It's a mess in there.'

It certainly was, Sally thought, listening to the list of drugs she'd had on the way in and mentally assessing her. Her left cheekbone was depressed, her eye seemed twisted slightly, her upper lip was huge and torn to ribbons and her lower jaw was grossly misshapen.

In fact, her face was so severely injured Sally was amazed that she hadn't had a lower score on the Glasgow coma scale, which measured the level of consciousness. She would have expected some degree of concussion, but maybe that would show itself later. She'd have to keep an eye on it and rescore her frequently.

In the meantime, her whole face was swelling before Sally's eyes, and she was getting restless, moving her head and fluttering her hands, fighting for breath.

It was a fair bet that the inside of her mouth was swelling too, cutting off her air supply. Protecting that had to be the first priority, and the moment she was on the trolley in Resus Sally was ready. 'Are you going to try and get an airway in?' she asked doubtfully, but Nick shook his head, confirming her suspicions.

'Not a chance, and we can't wait for the anaesthetist, she's distressed now. I'll do a laryngostomy. I don't want to poke about in there. OK, Jodie, just relax, you're in good hands. I'm just going to get you some air.'

Within seconds he'd located the cricothyroid membrane, made a neat little slit in it and slipped in a tube. Instantly the patient stopped struggling, and her colour started to improve in moments. 'Right, let's get some oxygen into her and assess her injuries. I want X-rays of head, chest, total spine and pelvis to start with, and we'll work from there. Is there a max-illofacial team here?'

'Yes—I've alerted them.'

'I want them here now. This needs urgent attention. Her eye socket's compressed and her tongue's bleeding badly. The orthopaedic reg could do with seeing her when we've got the plates, too, because this pelvis needs sorting out.'

They stood back as the radiographer slid the plates into the trolley, took the required shots and disappeared to develop them.

ABCDE, Sally thought. They'd sorted out her airway, made sure she was breathing, they were running in fluids to protect her circulation, Nick had done a brief neurological check to assess any obvious disability, and the last thing on the list was exposure—seeing the whole patient naked to check for anything else they might have missed. Before the door swung shut behind the radiographer, Sally was busy cutting clothes off, and it was immediately obvious that Jodie's pelvic injuries were very severe.

The skin over her hipbones was stained dark purple with bruises, and there were sharp spikes of bone pushing up against the skin in places.

'Nasty,' Nick said softly. 'The probability of internal injuries is very high, I think. Circulation to both legs seems good, though, amazingly. Watch her pressure—what is it?'

'A hundred over fifty.'

'She's young, but it's still very low. Watch it like a hawk, please. I don't want to miss anything. Pulse?'

'One-twenty and erratic.'

'She's breathing all right for herself still, so hopefully her spine's intact. Let's check her reflexes.'

He ran a quick neurological check to see if there was any likelihood of spinal damage, and incredibly she seemed to have been lucky. 'Looks OK. Wonders will never cease,' he murmured under his breath.

He gave her a little more pain relief, then bent over her, speaking clearly. 'OK, Jodie, I'm just going to have a look at your mouth and see what you've done,' he told her, then carefully removed the tape from the neck brace and opened her lower jaw a fraction to make sure there was nothing life-threatening that they'd yet to find. He was gentle, but of necessity thorough, and she moaned softly.

'Sorry, sweetheart,' he soothed. 'I won't be long.' He sucked out her mouth, his hands gentle as he probed the shattered jaw, and he shook his head.

'We need to tape this up to support it but there's nothing much to tape it to. She'll need it fixing a.s.a.p., and her tongue needs stitching fairly soon, it's still oozing. Where's the faciomaxillary surgeon, for heaven's sake?'

'Here.' The door slapped shut behind him, and he moved up beside Nick and assessed the patient rapidly. 'OK, I can see why you called me,' he said under his breath. 'Has she got a name?'

'Jodie Farmer.'

'Hello, Jodie, I'm Tom Kievenaar. Don't worry, we'll soon have you much more comfortable.' He turned back to Nick. 'Got any plates of this yet?'

'Right here,' the radiographer said, snapping them up onto the light box.

The evidence was incontrovertible. 'Ouch,' Nick said softly, and Tom gave a short, humourless laugh.

'Oh, yes, this one's a lulu. Lower jaw, upper jaw, cheekbone, nose, all the top front teeth—there's enough material here for a whole symposium. The rest of her skull looks all right, though, by a miracle. What's her GCS?'

'Fifteen at the scene, but she might have been KO'd. No deterioration since admission.'

'OK. No obvious neurological signs?'

Nick shook his head. 'Nothing so far.'

'Good—let's hope it stays like that. OK, let's get cracking. Anything else you've found out?'

'She's bitten her tongue—it's still bleeding slightly and it needs stitches, but it's not a priority. I haven't checked the spinal X-rays yet, though, so we need to do that before she's moved.'

They went over them together while Sally continued to monitor their patient and stabilise her. Her pressure was dropping slightly, probably due to the huge blood loss from her many fractures, and Sally opened up the flow on the plasma expander to maximum and reported the pressure drop to the two men.

'Is she cross-matched?' Tom asked, and Sally nodded.

'Six units on their way.'

'We'd better make it ten,' Nick said, running an eye rapidly over her again. 'Those pelvic injuries are worse than we'd thought.'

'They seem to have taken the brunt of the impact,' Tom murmured. 'The orthos might want to work at the other end while I do her face. I wouldn't want to move her too much until that lot's stabilised. Let's get some more plasma expander into her while we wait.'

It took a few more minutes before the orthopaedic registrar had come down and conferred with them, by which time the blood had arrived. Then Jodie was wheeled away and Sally felt the tension drain from her body as the responsibility for their patient passed on to the next team.

'Nasty mess,' Nick murmured, watching the trolley disappear through the double doors.

'Certainly is. I don't envy her. I wonder why she jumped?'

'I don't know, but the third floor isn't high enough, obviously. If you're going to do that, you need friends in higher places.'

'Or a friend with enough gumption to talk you out of it,' Sally said shortly, and stripped off her blood-streaked gloves and apron, dropping them into the bin. She glanced up at the clock and did a mild double-take. 'Good grief, is it really five-thirty?'

'Looks like it.'

She rolled her eyes. 'Marvellous. I finished at three.'

'Yes, I can see that,' Nick said with a grin.

'Oh, it's par for the course round here,' she assured

him. 'If I ever manage to get home before the rush hour, I'm doing well. I usually fail.'

'Such dedication to duty,' he teased, and she glowered at him, not in the mood to be criticised for doing her job properly.

'Don't knock it,' she advised tightly. 'Some of us have to be dedicated.'

He blinked and backed away a step. 'Ouch,' he murmured, his mouth twisting in a rueful smile. 'That wasn't criticism.'

'Better not have been,' she retorted, suppressing a twinge of guilt. 'Right, I'm going before anything else happens. I'll see you tomorrow.'

'How about a cup of tea first?' he suggested, but she shook her head. She was tempted—oh, how she was tempted—but she knew all about his charm. It was lethal, and she had absolutely no defences against it.

'I don't think so, not tonight. I've got to do some washing, I've got no clothes left.'

'Now that's an interesting thought,' he said softly, and his eyes caressed her, jamming the breath in her throat and draining the strength from her legs again.

'Forget it,' she advised, and walked away, resisting the urge to weaken and take him up on the offer of tea. All she needed now was to settle down with him for a cosy chat!

Little chats with Nick had a habit of getting much *too* cosy, and that lazy charm hadn't diminished over the years, not one iota. Besides, seeing him again after all this time had left her thoughts in turmoil, and she needed time alone to sort herself out.

Sally kept walking.

CHAPTER TWO

'So, you and Sally were quite close at one time, I gather?'

Nick flicked a quick glance at Ryan, but his expression was innocent. 'We were good friends,' he said guardedly, unsure what Sally might have told the Canadian consultant and unwilling to fuel hospital gossip at her expense—or his own, come to that.

On the other hand, he was perfectly willing to pump the man for anything he would reveal about Sally's life now.

'I haven't seen her for years,' he added with truth. 'It's good to see her looking so well and happy—I take it she is happy?'

'Yeah, she seems to be happy—and, no, I'm not going to tell you any more than that,' Ryan replied with a knowing smile. 'You want answers to questions, just ask her. I'm sure she'll tell you anything she wants you to know, she's usually pretty open.'

That sounded like his Sally, he thought with a pang of sadness. Open and honest and full of the joys of spring. Damn.

'What about you?' Ryan asked. 'Anyone in your life going to be affected by you two meeting up again like this? Strange coincidence, wasn't it?'

Nick gave a short huff of laughter. Ryan was altogether too smart.

'Wasn't it just?' he said noncommittally. 'But since you ask, no, there's no woman in my life.'

'And what about all the ghosts you've got behind you?' Ryan probed. 'Is it going to make it difficult for you two to work together?'

'No,' Nick said firmly. 'There won't be a problem.'

'I hope not,' he said, his voice mild but the warning there for all that. 'I don't want the department grinding to a halt because two of the main players are at each other's throats or weeping in the toilets.'

Nick's mouth kicked up in a grin as he crossed his fingers behind his back. 'I think you're safe—I'm not given to weeping in the toilets, and would you challenge Sally's temper?'

'Not knowingly,' Ryan admitted with a chuckle, and to Nick's relief the conversation moved onto safer topics. It had given him plenty to think about, though, and one thing in particular.

Ryan, despite the mild tone of his enquiries, was fiercely protective of Sally.

Fine. So was Nick. Just so long as Ryan didn't want her for himself...

'Nick was asking questions about you yesterday,' Ryan said quietly as they paused between patients.

Startled, Sally looked up and met his eyes. 'He was?'

Ryan nodded. 'I told him to ask you himself. I didn't want to tell tales.'

She shrugged, her heart thumping. He was asking about her? Was that good or bad? She picked up the next set of notes and glanced down at them, pretending interest.

'He was probably only being curious. We haven't seen each other for years,' she said, and Ryan nodded.

'Yeah, he said that. It could have been just idle curiosity.'

She shot him a quick glance. 'You don't think so, do you?' she asked, and Ryan shrugged.

'I don't know the man. You don't think he's a threat to you, Sally, do you?'

'A threat?' Oh, yes, he was a threat, but not in the sense Ryan meant. 'No,' she told Ryan. 'He's not a threat.' Not much. Her mouth dried, and she stared blindly at the notes. Only to her sanity—

'Sally? Those notes you're studying so avidly? They're upside down.'

She felt the colour run up her cheeks, and she turned on her heel and walked away from Ryan, cutting through to the waiting room to retrieve her next patient. Just by the door she paused, gathering her wits, and tried to put thoughts of him out of her mind.

It didn't matter that he was here, she told herself sternly. He was bound to ask questions about her, but it was irrelevant. Their affair was finished, over. She wasn't going to allow him to talk her into anything—not ever again.

'I've made coffee.'

Sally's hand flew up to cover her pounding heart, and she whirled on Nick. 'Will you not creep up on me!' she snarled furiously. 'You're going to give me a heart attack!'

His grin was unabashed. 'You'll get over it, you're made of sterner stuff than that.' He bent closer. 'I brought some really good Colombian coffee in—it's gorgeous. Come and have a cup.'

His voice was coaxing, and she could almost taste the coffee. She was parched, and they were fairly quiet, and she was overdue for a break...

'I'm only offering coffee,' he said in a gently teasing voice, and she felt soft colour brush her cheeks.

'I was just trying to work out if I'd got time,' she ad-libbed weakly.

'Liar. Come on, Sal, I'm not going to jump your bones. If you don't get in there soon the vultures will have descended on the pot and drained it.'

She summoned a smile. 'I'd better come now, then, hadn't I?'

'Dr Baker?'

They turned towards the voice of the young SHO, who was looking hopelessly out of his depth. 'Yes, Toby?'

'Um—I wonder if you could look at this X-ray for me, sir. I'm not sure if it's a fracture.'

Nick turned back to Sally and gave her a wry grin. 'Now you're definitely safe,' he murmured, and went into the cubicle, leaving her heading towards the staffroom with a sense of lingering disappointment that she was totally at a loss to understand.

There was still half a pot of coffee, and there was nobody in there, so she filled a mug, curled up in one of the chairs near the corner of the little room and rested her head against the back of the chair.

Bliss. The coffee smelt wonderful, and for a moment she was content just to inhale the aroma and relax. She hadn't slept well—too many painful memories churning, too much turbulent thought to be able to escape to oblivion. Seeing Nick again had stirred up a whole hornet's nest, and she felt edgy and restless and unhappy.

Still, for a moment she could relax. She opened her eyes, and jumped, almost slopping her coffee in her lap as she focused on him lounging against the worktop on the far side of the room.

'You've done it again!' she snapped, and he gave a wry grin.

'Sorry. I thought you were asleep. I was just contemplating my options.'

'Options?' she said suspiciously. 'What options?'

The smile was lazy. 'Foregoing the coffee and leaving you in peace, removing the cup so you didn't drown yourself in it when it tipped over, or waking you up. You've saved me from doing the wrong thing—unless just existing is enough to put me in your bad books?'

He looked so crestfallen she had to smile, even though she knew it was all an act.

'I'm awake,' she assured him, and he grinned and filled a mug, sitting down at right angles to her on the other side of the corner.

'How's the coffee?' he asked.

'I haven't tried it yet. I was getting high just smelling it.'

'You'll be glue-sniffing in a minute. Just drink it.'

She buried her nose in the mug, breathed again and tasted. 'Oh, gorgeous. You always could make good coffee.'

'Yours was always lousy, if I remember,' he said softly, and she could have kicked herself for bringing up the past.

'I've got better,' she said, firmly switching to the

present, and he let it go. Not for long, though, she was sure. She had a feeling Nick was headed for memory lane with her in tow, whether she wanted to go there or not.

And she didn't. The past was buried, her memories and her happiness and everything she cared for with it, and the last thing she needed was Nick dredging it all up again and throwing her life into chaos.

She drained her coffee, almost scalding her tongue and throat and not caring. 'Lovely,' she lied, not having tasted it in the end, and she unfolded her legs, stood up and tugged her dress straight. 'I have to fly. We aren't that quiet. Thanks for the coffee.'

She put her mug down and made her escape, leaving Nick to drink his coffee alone.

An hour later she was kicking herself. She shouldn't have said that about being quiet. They were never quiet, not this quiet, eerily so, as if the world had ground to a halt.

She grabbed the chance to do some teaching with her new nurses, told them to do a totally unnecessary stock-check of the stores and went round the waiting room, ripping down torn posters and sticking up fresh ones.

'Very pretty,' Nick said from behind her. 'How about a breath of fresh air? I've got some sandwiches from the trolley—care to join me?'

'I'm busy,' she lied, and he snorted.

'Sally, you've been killing time for the past hour. You have to eat, you may as well do it now.'

'Has it occurred to you that maybe I don't want to eat with you?' she snapped, and then regretted it when she saw the flicker of reproach in his eyes. 'I'm sorry,' she said with a sigh, too honest to lie to him, too kind to hurt him so casually. 'OK, I'll have lunch with you, just this once.'

'Such generosity,' he murmured drily, just to make her feel even worse!

They collected the sandwiches from his locker and filled fresh mugs with coffee, then headed out into the warm, humid August day. She led him round the corner of the building to a quiet, shady spot under the trees on the edge of a little garden. There was a bench there, and by a miracle there was nobody sitting on it.

'Perfect,' Nick said with a grin, and settled down, opening packets and offering them to her. 'Prawn salad and mayo, egg mayo or BLT?'

All her favourites. She sighed softly. 'Thank you,' she murmured, taking a prawn salad to start with and avoiding the knowing glint in his eye.

'So, tell me,' he said without preamble. 'What have you been up to for the past seven years?'

Getting over you, she thought, but that one was definitely staying private.

'Work, mostly. I've been here three years now, two as a junior sister, one as a G grade.'

'Still enjoying it?'

She nodded slowly, thoughtfully. 'Yes. It's tough—it's a difficult job, A and E. You see too much.'

'Tell me about it,' he said drily. 'I don't know why I went for it, except that it appealed to my sense of drama. I'm still an adrenaline junky, and I like making snap decisions and staying on my toes. It seemed to answer all the relevant criteria better than any other branch of medicine.'

That sounded like Nick. She remembered the dangerous sports he'd indulged in, the way he'd always driven just that tiny bit too fast for absolute safety—the times they'd failed to use contraception because they'd been somewhere unprepared and playing Russian roulette had appealed to him.

Except, of course, it hadn't been him who'd lost—

'Egg mayo?'

'Please,' Sally said, dragging her mind back to the present and safer territory. He held the packet out to her, and she eased the sandwich out, her fingers brushing his as she did so.

Heat shot up her arm, and she all but snatched the sandwich away and scooted further into the corner of the bench, taking her coffee with her and busying herself with eating and drinking for a minute to give her feelings time to subside.

Her body had other ideas, though. It remembered his touch, the caress of his hands, the feel of his body on hers. She closed her eyes, stifling a tiny moan of need.

No, she told herself firmly. He's bad news for you. You won't get over him again, it'll kill you. Just keep your distance.

'You look tired,' he said softly, and there was a thread of tender concern in his voice that nearly reduced her to tears.

'I am tired,' she confessed, swallowing the lump in her throat. She glanced at her watch and stood up. 'We need to go back. They don't know where we are, and I don't trust this quiet spell. All hell's going to break loose any minute, I just know it.'

Right on cue a siren sounded, and an ambulance swept out towards the gate, followed by another and another.

'Looks like trouble brewing,' Nick murmured. Scooping up the last of the sandwiches and wrappers, he dropped them in a bin and fell in beside her as she hurried round the corner, mugs in hand. The sirens were fading as they went through the doors, and the staff nurse in the triage room stuck her head out.

'Thank God you're back, they were about to page you. There's been a pile-up on the bypass near the Yarmouth Road roundabout—ten cars or something. At least fifteen casualties coming in, the police say, some serious. The worst are trapped and they want a medical team on the spot. Ryan wants you two to go.'

'OK,' she said, her blood pumping, her thoughts whirling. She ran down the corridor past Resus to the store, where Ryan was checking the emergency bag.

'Ah, you're here, good—right, Sally, take this lot. You'll need more fluids as well—there's another bag there. Don't think there's anything hazardous involved, it seems to be just cars, but apparently there was a diesel spill, so take care and keep out of it if you can. You'll need yellow coats—here, Nick, take this one.'

He handed him a coat with DOCTOR emblazoned across the back, and Sally grabbed her own off the back of the door.

'Do we have an exact location?' she asked, rapidly filling the other bag with fluids.

'East of the roundabout. Just head that way, I don't

think you can miss it, by all accounts. We'll contact you with more specific directions when we get them.' Ryan chucked Nick the keys of his car, and they ran out, jumped into it and headed out of the car park.

'You'll have to tell me where to go,' he said, cutting through the traffic with the siren wailing and the green light flashing on the roof.

She resisted the urge to make a smart remark, and directed him the quickest way out of the town and onto the bypass. Within five minutes Ambulance Control had contacted them with more specific directions, and ten minutes later, her heart in her mouth, Sally saw the first signs of the accident in the tailback ahead.

'Siren again, I think,' Nick said, and shot her a grim smile. 'It's a pity that the only time I ever get to do this, I'm too busy thinking about what we might find to enjoy the power trip.'

The traffic seemed to melt away in front of them, cars squeezing up onto the verges and pulling over to let them through, and then they were there in the thick of it, surrounded by flashing lights and screams and sobs and shouted commands. People were wandering around aimlessly, obviously in shock, and some of them were bleeding from head wounds.

'OK, let's see what the problems are,' Nick said, hoisting the heavier of the bags into his arms and running towards the ambulance teams.

'What have you got for us?' he asked, shrugging into his coat, and the man in charge directed them towards the centre of the carnage.

'We can handle the walking wounded for now,' he said, 'but we've got a couple of entrapments that need

your help. That blue Fiesta is the worst, I believe, and
the red BMW is the other one.'

Sally looked the way he was pointing, and saw a
car just like hers with the nose tucked under the side
of a lorry. The roof was crushed in, and she gave a
little shudder. It was a little close to home.

They walked quickly over there. A paramedic was
half in, half out of the back window of the car, con-
torted into an impossible position, and while Sally
tried not to shudder at the state of the car, Nick squat-
ted down and spoke to him.

'I think this lady's got a tension pneumothorax, but
I'm too big to do anything about it,' he said over his
shoulder. 'There's no room to move. Hang on, I'll
come out.'

He squirmed out backwards, and looked assess-
ingly at them both. 'You could get in,' he said to
Sally, and she nodded, suppressing her feelings.

'OK. What do you want me to do, Nick?'

'Check her for signs of pneumothorax or cardiac
tamponade,' he said. 'Has she got oxygen?'

The paramedic nodded. 'Yes. She's in pain, but I
didn't want to give her anything that would lower her
blood pressure. The steering-wheel's rammed into her
chest. She's bound to have internal injuries.'

'Where are the fire brigade? They should be cutting
her out.'

'They're here—they're working on the other en-
trapment. He's got severe bleeding from the leg.
We're bagging in fluids but we're only just holding
him. We've assessed them all for priority but you
might want to reassess them in a minute. There was

a doctor in one of the cars, he's giving us a hand, too.'

'Where does this one come in the priority list?' Nick asked, jerking his head towards the Fiesta.

'The top at the moment. The other guy's grim but, like I said we're holding him for the minute, and we've got two fatalities, but this lady's going to join them if you can't do something soon.'

'I'll go in,' Sally said. 'You can pass me the things I need.'

She hated small spaces, but there were times when you just had to forget about things like that. She squirmed through the narrow opening left by the bent roof, and laid her hand on the lady's shoulder.

She moaned and turned her head towards Sally, but she couldn't speak.

'It's all right, I'm going to help you,' Sally said with a quick squeeze to her shoulder. Talking softly to reassure her patient, she rapidly checked her symptoms.

The woman had distended jugular veins, which meant that the blood vessels in her chest were being compressed and causing a build-up of pressure. Her chest seemed distended on the left side, although it moved less when she breathed in and out, and she was restless and her pulse was rapid. The picture was consistent with a lung leaking air into the chest and collapsing the lungs—rapidly fatal if left untreated.

Sally turned her head and reported to Nick. 'I think it is a tension pneumothorax,' she said. 'The signs all fit. She's looking pretty rough.' She ran through the symptoms and he nodded.

'Certainly sounds like it. Can you get enough access to do a decompression?'

She looked at the woman's chest. The simple answer was no, but the simple answer meant that she'd die. 'Yes, I can do it,' she said firmly. If she could just get the needle in at the right angle...

'OK. I'll talk you through it. Find the second or fourth intercostal space, and insert the needle along the upper border of the rib. Don't go below it, you'll get the artery and nerve. I'll hand you the needle and a wipe now.'

'Pass me scissors first, her blouse is in the way,' she said, and, taking them, she sliced away the clothes over the woman's collar-bone and then handed them back. 'Right, let's have a wipe and the needle.'

He talked her through it, and seconds later there was a little pop, and a rush of air through the end of the cannula.

'OK, can you slide the catheter in now and take the needle out?' he asked, and when she'd done that and had checked it was still venting, she taped it in place and wriggled back out.

'She's looking better,' she said, 'but she needs to come out of there fast. I don't think I can do anything else in there, the space is too tight.'

Nick nodded, and hailed the fire brigade officer who was in charge of freeing the casualties. 'We need to get this lady out fast.'

'Give me ten more minutes and we'll be with you. Can she last that long?'

Sally shrugged. 'I hope so.'

'We need to reassess the others,' Nick said briskly.

'Status can change very rapidly under these conditions.'

Just then they were hailed by the paramedic working on the person with the trapped and bleeding leg, and they had no choice but to leave their lady with the pneumothorax. With a last glance over her shoulder, Sally followed Nick and found herself down in the passenger footwell of the BMW, applying a compression bandage to the lacerated limb to try and prevent any further blood loss while the fire brigade worked on the bulkhead with the air cutters.

It was only a few moments before he was released, and then Nick left the other casualties he was treating and came over to supervise his extraction from the car and make sure he was stable before he was whisked away to hospital.

Most of the casualties were suffering from cuts and bruises, and some were dealt with on the spot by the ambulance staff and taken to hospital for a routine check-up; others went straight off in the ambulances for treatment of fractures and stitching of lacerations once their condition was known to be stable.

Once the critical patients were dealt with, Nick and Sally turned their attention to the noisy ones—anyone who could make a fuss was going to live at least a few more minutes, and they worked their way through them as rapidly as possible.

The lady with the pneumothorax was freed after half an hour, and they broke off to supervise her removal and dispatch before going back to the less seriously injured.

Finally everyone had been dealt with, and Nick straightened up and stripped off his gloves, scrubbing his face on his shoulder in a weary gesture that tugged at Sally's heartstrings.

'Well, at least we didn't lose anyone else,' she said softly, and he nodded.

'I know. Right, we need to get back to the unit. No doubt they'll be in chaos.'

They stripped off their yellow coats and stashed them in the boot, along with the depleted bags of emergency supplies, and then Nick reversed back out of the wreckage that surrounded them and they drove slowly away, leaving the police to clear the crumpled cars away and get the road open.

'It's nearly five again,' he said to her as they pulled up outside the hospital a short while later.

Sally sighed. 'I know. Maybe one day I'll knock off on time.'

'I shouldn't hold your breath,' he said with a chuckle, and she smiled wryly.

'Don't worry, I'm not. I wonder if they still need me, or if I can get away?'

Nick cut the engine and looked across at her, then reached out and brushed his knuckles across her cheek. 'Nobody's indispensable, Sal,' he said softly. 'Why don't you go home? You look all in.'

She dragged her eyes from his and turned away, reaching blindly for the doorhandle. 'I'm fine. I want to make sure my pneumothorax lady is OK before I go, if I do nothing else.'

'OK, but then you go,' he said firmly.

She made a noncommittal noise and opened the door, climbing out and looking towards the doors. The waiting room was full, no doubt with people who'd been delayed because of the crash and put to the back of the queue. If she stayed, she could help them get through the backlog quicker—

'No.'

He'd appeared beside her; she glanced up into his face and saw his eyes were filled with gentle understanding. 'No, what?' she asked defensively. 'I'm my own boss, Nick.'

'You always were,' he reminded her, and there was a thread of reproach in his voice.

She felt a twinge of guilt, and then reminded herself of the facts. 'I only refused to move to Manchester with you because our relationship was going nowhere.'

'Was it? I didn't know where it was going. I wanted to find out. It was *you* who didn't care.'

'I cared!' she exclaimed. 'You told me to forget it, because I wouldn't drop everything and go with you to the other end of the country! And then, when I tried to contact you, you didn't bother to ring.'

He paused, his eyes searching. 'I did try and ring,' he said quietly. 'I tried that number you gave me several times. Nobody had ever heard of a Staff Nurse Clarke. I assumed, in the end, that you must have been working for an agency, so I rang all the agencies I could get hold of. None of them had a Sally Clarke registered with them. I didn't understand. I thought, if it was important enough, you'd ring me again—but you didn't.'

She looked away, her heart pounding. She didn't need this conversation—not now, when she was tired and stressed and pulled in all directions.

'So what happened, Sal?' he asked. 'Where were you? How did you disappear?'

'I—left,' she lied, and opened the boot, hauling out bags. 'Come on, we need to get inside and make ourselves useful.'

'You're avoiding me.'

It wasn't a question, so she didn't bother to answer. She just picked up a bag, slung the straps over her shoulder and headed off towards A and E, leaving Nick behind her to deal with the other bag.

After a second she heard the boot lid slam and the click of the central locking, and his firm, crisp footsteps followed her. As they reached the door he grasped her arm and turned her towards him, his eyes glittering with determination.

'Sally, I want to know. Why did you ring me—and why did you disappear?'

His voice was controlled, but he was angry, she could tell—angry and not about to be fobbed off again. She had to give him something, so she gave him a carefully doctored version of the truth.

'I wanted to speak to you,' she said evenly, avoiding those piercing blue eyes. 'A member of my family was in hospital—I just needed to talk to you. I didn't contact you again because it didn't matter any more. It was no longer relevant.'

One of the nurses hailed them, and she turned away and pulled her arm back. 'Come on, we're needed,' she told him, and headed through the doors.

'What do you mean, no longer relevant?' he asked, pulling her to a halt again.

Sally swallowed and forced herself to meet his eyes, praying that the emotion she was feeling didn't show.

'She died.'

He sighed and thrust a hand through his hair. 'Oh, Sal, I'm sorry. Someone special?'

She rammed down the huge wave of pain that threatened to rise up and swamp her.

'Yes. Very special,' she said honestly, and turned away, blinded by sudden tears. 'Very special,' she repeated in a whisper, and all but ran away from him down the corridor to the stores.

There she dumped the bag, hung her coat up on the peg and headed back out to the work station. Angela, the senior sister, was there, filling out notes, and she looked up and smiled distractedly.

'Good grief, Sally, isn't it time you went home?' she asked.

'Do you need me?

The smile softened. 'We always need you, but you look bushed.' Her eyes narrowed. 'In fact, you look like hell. Go home. Have a nice strong whisky in the bath—it'll do you good.'

'I might do that,' Sally said with a vain attempt at a smile. 'How's my pneumothorax?'

'Doing fine. She's gone up to the ward.'

'Good. Right, I'll go, then.' She fumbled her things out of the locker in the staffroom and headed for the door, only to find Nick standing in her way.

'Not now, please,' she said wearily, right at the end of her tether.

'When, then? Tomorrow? The next day? Or never?'

She closed her eyes, her control hanging by a thread. 'Please, Nick,' she begged, and she felt his hands close over her arms and support her.

'Sweetheart, are you all right?' he asked gruffly, and she felt the unwanted tears welling again.

'I'm fine,' she said, a little choked. 'Just tired. Let me go, Nick.'

Slowly, reluctantly, he released her, and she all but ran to her car, driving away as quickly as the traffic would allow. She held on until she got home, until the door closed behind her, and then finally the dam burst.

CHAPTER THREE

TROUBLED, Nick watched Sally go, not at all convinced that he believed her story—or at least, not all of it, and not in the form in which it had been presented to him.

There was something she wasn't telling him—something major, something that had torn her apart. He knew her too well to be fobbed off, just as he knew she was hurting now.

'Ah, Nick, just the guy I was looking for,' Ryan said, coming up behind him. 'Could I put you in charge of the waiting-room contingent? I think we're OK on the RTA now, it's just tidying up, but that lot in there could use some fast professional decision-making and they're a bit short-handed—Toby's rather out of his depth. You want to handle it for me?'

'Sure. I reek of diesel, though—I ended up kneeling in it. I need a minute to change.'

'I don't suppose they'll even notice,' Ryan assured him.

Dragging his eyes from the door, he nodded and went in search of a white coat and clean trousers. He couldn't deal with Sally until later and, besides, he didn't have her address. He'd have to find a way to wheedle it out of someone—but who? Ryan would never give it to him, always assuming he knew it anyway, but one of the girls might if he used his charm.

He smiled grimly. It was unfair and unethical, but there were times, like this, when that was just tough. He headed for the waiting room and bided his time.

It wasn't hard, in the end. As he was finishing off, he simply asked Angela, the senior sister on duty, if she had Sally's phone number. 'She left something in Ryan's car, and I don't know if she needs it. I thought I'd ring her—if it's important I could drop it round to her on my way home.' He cranked up the charm, and she crumpled like a paper bag.

Stage one, he thought, pocketing the number. Now for the telephone directory. He looked up Clarke, scanned down the 'S's until he found her number and, bingo, he had her address.

Excellent. All he had to do now was find it, and a walking road map strolled into the department at that point. With a grim smile, he approached the policeman and showed him the road name.

'It's a colleague—I have to drop something round there and I don't know the area. I wonder if you could direct me?'

'Sure. Know the Old London Road? It's off there—small, fairly new development. You can't miss it.'

He shook his head. 'Sorry. I'm new here. I wouldn't know where to start.'

'No matter, I'll jot it down for you.' The policeman took the piece of paper with Sally's address on it and sketched out a neat map. 'There you go, that should get you there.'

Nick wondered if the small victory showed in his eyes. 'Cheers, mate,' he said, clapping the man on the shoulder, and within minutes he was on his way.

He dived home first and showered and changed to wash the smell of blood and diesel off his skin, and then, dressed in clean jeans and a polo shirt, he checked the sketch map against his road atlas, got back in the car and set off.

It was impossible to miss, as the policeman had said, but a real maze. Still, at least it was well lit and he could see the road names clearly. He turned into Sally's road, crawled along until he spotted her number and pulled over, studying it for a moment.

It was a pleasant little house, he thought. Neat, tidy, nothing fantastic, but there were trees in the street and it looked a decent neighbourhood. The house was semi-detached, but staggered so that only part of it was linked to the next house, and it gave the illusion of more privacy.

There was a car on the drive, a sensible little navy blue Fiesta not quite in its first flush of youth, exactly the sort of car he pictured her driving—exactly like the car the injured woman had been trapped in today. Had it worried her? Very likely.

Pondering his reception, he got out of his car and approached the house. There were lights on at the back, but the hall was dark behind the glass door and the outside light remained firmly unlit. He rang the doorbell and wondered idly if she owned the house. Probably. She'd always wanted security. She would have bought one by now, he was almost sure of it, and this was probably within her reach.

The hall light came on, and through the glass he saw a figure approaching. She opened the door and looked up at him, and her face hardened.

'Nick, no,' she said, trying to shut the door, but the

pain in her eyes was more than he could bear and he eased the door open and went in, closing it softly behind him.

She turned away and he followed her, catching her shoulders and turning her gently to face him. Her eyes were red-rimmed and puffy, but she held his gaze defiantly.

'I don't recall inviting you in,' she said, and her voice was cold. 'You might like to leave before I call the police.'

A sensible man would have walked away, but Nick had never been sensible where Sally was concerned. He shook his head.

'Sal, talk to me,' he urged. 'What is it? What's wrong?'

'Nothing's wrong, except that you're standing in my hall and I want you to leave.'

He shook his head and frowned. 'Don't change the subject, you know what I mean. What happened all those years ago that made you ring me?'

For an age she hesitated, as if she was engaged in some internal struggle, then the fight seemed to go out of her.

'I had a baby,' she said, so quietly that for a moment he wondered if he'd heard her right.

Then the impact of her words hit home, and he stared at her in shock. 'A baby?' he echoed. He sucked in some much-needed air. 'You mean I'm a father? All these years I've been a father and I didn't even *know*?'

Sally shook her head. 'You're not a father,' she told him.

Anger shot through him, and he had to forcibly

restrain himself. 'What the hell do you mean, I'm not a father? Is this one of these pedantic statements about biological function not inferring automatic rights, or are you telling me it's not my child?' he bit out furiously.

'Oh, she was yours all right,' Sally confirmed, and then went on, her gentle voice tinged with bitterness, 'She died, Nick. That's why I rang you—to tell you she was dying—but you didn't call me.'

Shock drained the strength from his legs for a moment, and he stood stock still, hanging on to reality by a thread.

'My God,' he said eventually, his voice rising. 'All these years you've kept this secret and you never even bothered to tell me?'

'What was the point?' she blazed. 'She was dead, Nick! There was nothing to be achieved by contacting you and, besides, you didn't care anyway or you would have rung me. By the time she was dead it was too late—too late for everything!'

She turned away, and this time he let her go. He was too stunned to follow her, too stunned and shocked and...

Gutted. He felt utterly gutted. He'd had a child, and he'd never seen her, never felt her move in her mother's womb, never touched her, never held her, and now it was too late—nearly seven years too late, and all because a phone message hadn't got to him in time.

Nick sank back against the wall and closed his eyes, dragging his hand over his face. He stayed there for an age, staring into space, thoughts reeling through his head.

Thoughts, and then questions. Endless questions. And guilt.

He could hear the clink of crockery coming from the kitchen and, shrugging away from the wall, he followed the sounds.

He still looked stunned, Sally thought. Stunned and wounded, but no longer angry.

Good. This wasn't an area in which she could cope with his anger. It was a very private part of her, a part she'd dealt with alone. Sharing it at all was going to be very, very difficult.

'I'm sorry,' he said gruffly, and she jerked her head up and stared at him in amazement.

'Sorry?' she echoed.

'That I didn't contact you. I was away. My father had been taken into hospital—he had angina. I was at home for the weekend. My house-mate didn't give me your message until Wednesday. I don't suppose he realised it was urgent or he would have given you my home number.'

Of course, it had been the weekend. 'It was Saturday morning,' she said, feeling hollow as she remembered.

'When…?' He trailed off, searching her face help-lessly. 'When did she…?'

She knew what he was asking, what he couldn't find the words to say. 'Saturday afternoon, a quarter to five,' she told him gently, then went on, 'She had an inoperable congenital deformity of her heart, and she was too weak for a transplant, even if a donor heart had been available. There was never any hope. I knew that, from the moment I saw her.'

Nick nodded, understanding, and then looked up at her again, his eyes anguished. 'I'm sorry—I should have been there for you. It must have been hell.'

Sally looked away, swallowing the lump in her throat. 'It was,' she admitted. 'I went into labour early—I was about thirty-two weeks. They said it would probably be all right, and they tried to slow me down, but it didn't work. I had her at six on Saturday morning, and I rang you at eight or thereabouts, when the shock had worn off a little and I realised you should see her. You didn't ring back—I assumed you didn't care.'

'I didn't know.'

'I realise that now, but then it never occurred to me that you might not have got the message, not till much later, and there didn't seem any point then in contacting you. I knew you'd be hurt. There didn't seem to be any reason to do it.'

'And if she'd been all right?' he asked, an edge in his voice again. 'Would you have contacted me then? Or would you have brought her up alone?'

'I don't know,' she said honestly. 'I hadn't decided. You'd walked away, told me there was no future for us—'

'No,' he corrected. 'I told you I wasn't ready for marriage. I told you we were too young to make a commitment at that stage and I didn't want a long-distance affair. I never said we didn't have a future.'

'And if I'd told you about the baby, what then? Would you have married me out of duty? I didn't want that, Nick.'

He rammed his hands into his pockets and looked away. He was silent for an age, and then he spoke, the words seemingly dragged from him. 'Did you give her a name?'

'Amy. It means beloved.'

His eyes fluttered shut, and his jaw worked restlessly for a moment.

Sally went on, 'I've got pictures of her, and I kept her clothes. They also took hand-and footprints for me. I thought...if you were too late, you might want to see them. They're upstairs. I'll show you.'

He followed her, sitting on the bed in the spare room and staring in silence at each of the little things she showed him—the tiny handprint, the premature-size sleepsuit which had all but drowned her, the photographs of her in Sally's arms.

His jaw worked, and a silent tear slid down his cheek. She laid a hand gently on his shoulder and stood up.

'I'll be downstairs,' she said, and left him alone to grieve for the daughter he'd never known.

Nick appeared silently in the doorway, but Sally knew he was there. His face was grave, his eyes sombre.

'Coffee?' she offered, and he nodded.

'Please.'

She went through to the kitchen and made him a cup of instant coffee. She didn't even attempt the real thing. As he'd reminded her, she made lousy coffee.

She put the mug in his hand and searched his face, and he gave her a crooked smile. 'It's OK, Sally,' he murmured. 'I'm all right. It's just a lot to take in.'

'I know. I've had years to get used to it. Have you eaten?'

He shook his head, and before she could stop herself, she'd offered to cook for him. Fool, she thought. Get him out!

But she couldn't. The offer had been made and accepted, and the best she could hope for was that he wouldn't settle in for the whole evening. She really, really didn't think she could deal with that.

He didn't stay long. A part of him wanted to, but another, larger part needed to be alone to assimilate his thoughts and finish dealing with the bombshell she'd landed on him.

She made pasta in a garlicky tomato sauce with cheese on top, quick and simple and delicious, and it was cosily domestic and curiously heart-rending and familiar.

They'd had all this, and they'd thrown it away because of a few ill-judged words and an excess of pride. Idiots, he thought. If only he'd been more patient, if only she hadn't told him to go to hell...

So many if onlys. Too many.

He helped her wash up, desperately trying to ignore the scent of her hair as she leant across him to put a plate in the sink, the feel of her body nudging his. He ached for her, but he was used to that, and tonight, of all nights, wasn't the time.

When the last dish was put away, she turned to him with a smile that didn't quite reach her eyes. 'Coffee?' she offered, but he knew she was only being polite and, anyway, he needed space.

'No, I'll be getting on,' he said. She followed him to the front door and reached for the latch. He stopped her, laying his hand over hers.

'Thank you for telling me about Amy and showing

me the things,' he said softly. 'I realise it must be difficult for you.'

Her eyes shimmered a little. 'You're welcome. I'm sorry it was such a shock.'

He gave a hollow laugh. 'It would have been a shock seven years ago, Sal,' he pointed out. 'Only maybe then I would have been of some use to you.'

He lifted his other hand, the one that wasn't holding hers on the latch, and brushed his knuckles over her cheek. 'Sleep tight,' he murmured, and, bending his head, he touched his lips briefly to hers. They were soft and warm and yielding, and the ache intensified.

He pulled away before he gave in to temptation, and opened the door. 'I'll see you tomorrow,' he said, his voice gruff, and strode down the path to his car without looking back. At the end of the road he stopped, turned round, stared at her house.

Temptation was a dangerous thing, and he was very, very tempted. Still, tonight wasn't the night, not for either of them. He went back to his motel and stared at the ceiling for hours, then finally, just before dawn, he fell asleep.

'Oh, dear, not you again, Martin!'

The young lad grinned at Sally and hopped into the cubicle. 'Sorry, Sister. It just—'

'Went,' they said together, and laughed.

'Is your mum with you today?' she asked, and he shook his head.

'No. I was in the park playing football—a mate gave me a lift. I'll tell her later—when I'm all bandaged up and she doesn't have to stress. It's bad enough on my own, without her getting upset when I yell.'

She laughed and helped him up onto the examination couch. 'You lie here, I'll get Dr Baker to come and sort you out.'

Martin reached out and grabbed her arm. 'Sister—is he OK?'

Remembering the last time, Sally nodded. 'Yes, Martin, he's good,' she told him, and crossed her fingers. 'He's done it loads of times.' She slipped out of the cubicle and went up to Nick at the work station.

'Can I borrow you for a sec?' she asked quietly. 'Recurrent dislocation of the patella—Martin knows the form. Only, can you do it cleanly? His last experience was a bit rough.'

Nick nodded. 'Sure.' He followed her back in and perched on the edge of the couch.

'Hi,' he said with a grin. 'I'm Dr Nick Baker. I gather this is a habit of yours?'

Martin rolled his eyes. 'You could say that.'

'Have you seen the orthopaedic team about it?'

'Yeah—they said they'd do something if it got too bad, but they don't want to yet. They keep trying to train me not to do whatever triggers it, but it seems to happen easier and easier.'

Nick pulled a wry face and looked down at the knee. It was bent slightly, the kneecap pushed out to the outside, and from Martin's apprehensive face it was obvious he knew exactly what was coming.

Sally handed him the Entonox mask and he took several deep breaths, propping himself up on his elbows and looking down at his knee. Then he glanced at Nick and nodded.

'OK. Just do it.'

'It'll be fine,' Nick said confidently. Sally wasn't so sure. The last time the doctor on duty had had two goes at reducing it, and Martin had been in agony.

She should have had more faith, she thought a second later. Nick had grasped Martin's ankle, pressed firmly on the side of his kneecap and gently but steadily pulled his leg straight. There was an audible plop, and the patella dropped neatly into place.

Martin yelped, and then laughed with relief, and Sally left him breathing from the mask for a moment until the pain had subsided.

'Oh, that's so much better,' the lad said weakly, and chuckled. 'I thought it was going to be like last time.'

Nick grinned and flexed his hands. 'It's all down to the wrist action,' he said with a grin. 'Now, I don't think it needs another X-ray, I expect you've had so many your leg glows in the dark. I think we'll just put a pressure bandage on it to stop it slipping again and refer you to the orthopaedic surgeons for reassessment. It might be time to consider surgery, but they'll decide. In the meantime, no more football for a while, please, and you need a knee support with a hole in it to locate the patella.'

'I've got one of those.'

'So wear it!' Nick admonished.

'Yes, sir!'

'That's better.'

He grinned at the lad, and Martin chuckled again and sat up cautiously.

'Stay there, I'll bandage it,' Sally told him, and he leant back on his hands and looked down at the swollen and discoloured knee. 'I suppose I could ring my mum,' he said, and sighed. 'She'll stress at me.'

'It was hardly deliberate,' Sally reminded him with a smile. 'And it's only because she loves you.'

'No accounting for taste,' Nick said with a wink, and headed out of the cubicle to his next patient, leaving Sally to finish Martin's bandaging off and listen to the young man waxing lyrical about Nick's amazing skill.

Sally found herself agreeing. She'd seen him on the previous two days working under pressure, calmly making rapid and accurate assessments of severely injured patients, working steadily to stabilise them without drama and haste, and yet getting everything done as necessary.

That was a rare gift. To be able to do something simple like pop a kneecap back so deftly into place in a young lad who knew only too well how painful it could be took a whole different set of skills, and clearly he had them, too.

Blast. She didn't need to add admiration of his professional qualities to her already long list of reasons for falling for him! She needed distance. She needed to be able to look at him and think, He's just an ordinary man.

She didn't need him to be anything special, to stand out from the crowd and make himself any more desirable to her. It had been bad enough *before* she knew how good a doctor he'd be. Now it was next to impossible.

She sighed and cleared up the cubicle, and found herself wondering if Nick had had any sleep last night or if he routinely had bags under his eyes these days.

He'd looked tired, she thought, and a little pensive. Because of Amy? Or because of her?

Amy, probably. He hadn't wanted to stay for coffee last night after their simple meal, even when she'd offered to let him make it. Stupidly, perversely, that had hurt.

She was nuts. She didn't want to encourage him. Last night when he'd turned up, he'd been the last person in the world she'd wanted to see.

What she needed was a personal stereo, with a constantly running loop of tape reminding her of all the reasons why he was bad news.

All she had to do was remember what they were and she'd be fine...

It was a long old day, Nick thought. A long old day after a singularly long and unrefreshing night. And tonight probably wouldn't be any better. Since he'd seen Sally again, all his sleep was filled with dreams of her. Still, he might be having nightmares about his house purchase tonight instead, if the solicitor hadn't got his finger out yet.

He finished work at six, drove back to his motel and phoned the 24-hour conveyancing firm who were handling his house purchase.

'Any joy?' he asked them, and was told that the sale had been completed at noon and the house was now his.

'The keys are with the neighbour,' the solicitor told him. 'You can collect them any time you like. The services have been left on and the meters read, so you've got light and water and the phone all ready for you.'

'Excellent,' he said, and, after discussing a few last details, he hung up, paused for a moment and pulled a piece of paper out of his pocket.

She'd probably say no. She would if she had any sense, at least. With a rough sigh, he stabbed in her number and waited.

She must be mad. Why on earth had she agreed to go and see his house with him? She didn't *care* where Nick lived, didn't want to know. She didn't want to be able to picture him in it, or know where it was so she could drive past in the night and see if his lights were still on.

Been there, done that, she thought heavily.

And yet here she was, waiting for him by her front door, her eyes fixed on the point in the road where his car would appear, and her tongue was all but hanging out! Stupid girl. Stupid, stupid girl—

There he was. The car coasted to a halt beside her and he leant over and opened the door. 'Hi, there,' he said with a grin. 'All set?'

Sally nodded, trying to remind herself that sparkling blue eyes and a sexy grin didn't make him a reliable person. He'd walked out on their relationship before, he could do it again.

This was just friendship—one friend going with another to see his new house and express a little *friendly* interest.

Nothing else.

So why, she thought as she slid in beside him and fastened her seat belt, did it feel so very much like a date?

'I need to get the key off the neighbour first. I've

rung her, and she's in. I just hope she isn't incurably nosy.'

'Bound to be. It's human nature.' And I'm here to fuel the gossip, she thought with a sinking heart. Oh, well.

Nick's new house was in a nicely established village-style development a few minutes from the hospital side of the town, in a very pleasant but fairly modest road fringed with trees. The houses varied from large detached executive-types to semis and little bungalows; it was an interesting mix, and the small detached house on the corner outside which he pulled up seemed at first glance much like one or two of the other middle-of-the-range houses she could see.

Then through the trees she noticed the large hexagonal extension on the back, tall windows almost filling three sides of it and stretching from floor to ceiling. Her interest aroused, she lurked restlessly outside the garden fence while he went to retrieve the keys, trying to peer through without being too conspicuous and wishing he'd hurry up.

After what seemed like an age he came back with a broad grin and a keyring dangling from his fingers, and let them in.

'Welcome to *chez moi*,' he said with a wry smile, and looked around him.

'As you remember it?' she asked, recalling that her own house hadn't been.

'Pretty much,' he murmured, running his fingers experimentally over the banister rail. 'Come and have a guided tour.'

Nick led her down the long hall past the stairs and into the sitting room, an L-shaped room with patio doors out to the garden and a bookcase wall that she positively envied him. She still had boxes of books in a spare bedroom waiting for a shelf to put them on.

'Nice room,' she said, looking round. 'The carpets and curtains seem all right.'

He shrugged. 'They're not in their first flush of youth, but they'll do for a while. At least the decor's neutral. Come on, I want to show you the rest.'

'What's through there?' she asked, indicating another door.

'Uh-uh,' he said, propelling her gently back into the hall. 'I'm saving that till last. Upstairs.'

She ran up, looking round the three perfectly ordinary and decent bedrooms and the bathroom with its gleaming white suite.

'Looks new.'

'It is,' he told her. 'The previous owners only did it six months ago, and then she got pregnant again and they decided they needed a bigger house. They've got three children already.'

Lucky them, Sally thought. 'I can see why they'd be a bit crowded. How do you get to the other bedroom?'

'It's only got three.'

'But—the bit at the back...'

He gave a cheeky grin and tapped the side of his nose. 'All in good time,' he said, and led her downstairs and through the galley kitchen to the hexagonal room that had caught her attention.

It was just as interesting as she'd expected, like walking into a huge Victorian bay window with the walls set at forty-five degrees, and because the windows filled the walls and came right down to floor level, it really seemed to be a part of the garden. It had a lovely feel, and in the corner was the answer to her question.

'A spiral staircase!' she said, finally understanding. 'I was wondering if it didn't have an upstairs but just a huge vaulted ceiling, and it seemed such a waste, but I couldn't work out how you'd get to it. So is it another bedroom?'

'No, it's my study, and it's the reason I bought the house,' he told her with a grin. He waved an arm at the stairs. 'Go on up.'

She went, and found herself in a wonderful room with another wall of fitted bookshelves on one side and the fabulous floor-to-ceiling windows on the other.

The branches of a birch tree outside grazed the glass like a natural net curtain and lent the room a wonderful air of seclusion.

'Oh, it's gorgeous, it's like being in a tree-house!' she said, and turned to him with a smile. 'Now I'm very definitely jealous!'

'Tough, it's mine,' he said, his smile smug, but his eyes held a strange expression that made her feel strangely sad. After a second he looked away, drawing in a deep breath and looking round the room in satisfaction.

'It's going to be wonderful to have a proper study,' he said after a moment. 'I've got so much work to do for my exams, and it will be brilliant to be able to come up here and get on with it in amongst the tree-tops.'

'You always were a tree-hugger,' she teased, but he shook his head.

'I don't have time to look at the trees,' he said with a wry smile. 'More's the pity. I don't have much time for anything.'

'Oh, poor baby,' she said, still teasing, and he rolled his eyes.

'Come on, let's go down and put the kettle on.'

'Is there one?' she asked doubtfully. She hadn't seen one in passing, but their tour of the kitchen had been brief to say the least!

'There is in my car.' He went out and came back with a couple of carrier bags. After unpacking the kettle and other goodies, he filled it and plugged it in.

'There's a card here,' she told him, waving a brightly coloured envelope at him. 'It was propped up on the worktop. From the previous people, I suppose. It's addressed to you.'

Sally handed him the envelope, and he slit it open and read it, then smiled.

'How kind. Here, have a look. You can stick it up on the shelves in the sitting room—it can be my first ornament.'

She scanned the card, just a simple straightforward 'Welcome to your New Home' type of card, but inside they'd written, 'Hope you're as happy here as we have been. Good luck with your dreams. Jo and Ross.'

'Isn't that sweet of them?' she murmured, and wondered what dreams he had, and if Jo and Ross had known about them. She went through to the sitting room and put it in the middle of the shelves. When she turned round he was standing right behind her.

'It's a little lonely,' he said with a crooked smile, and then looked down at her, his eyes tracking her face. 'So, what do you think of the house?' he asked, collecting himself visibly after a breathless second.

Sally ignored the thump of her heart and returned his smile. 'I like it. It's got a nice atmosphere—friendly. And I could hate you for the study, it's gorgeous!'

Nick's grin widened. 'If you're very good and promise not to make a mess, I'll let you come and sit in it from time to time.'

'You're so kind. Am I supposed to be grateful?'

'Try honoured.'

She poked her tongue out at him and went back into the kitchen.

'Tea or coffee?' she asked, and he elbowed her out of the way.

'Coffee—and I'm making it.'

Just like old times, she thought, the teasing banter, the arguments over the coffee.

Except tonight, of course, wouldn't end as those nights had ended. Regret washed over her, and she pushed it aside.

'So where are the chocolate biscuits?' she asked with false cheer, and he gave a theatrical sigh and dug about in the bag, tossing a packet of plain chocolate digestives at her.

'You thought I'd forgotten, didn't you?' he asked, and she looked up from struggling with the packet and dredged up a grin.

'Not a chance. You're too much of a pig—and I seem to remember you always ate most of them.'

'I'm sure I didn't.'

'You did. You dunked them.'

Sally's heart ached with the memory. They'd always had chocolate biscuits with their coffee in the evening, and it had always been Nick's job to get them. It had become a nightly ritual, a prelude to their other nightly rituals, like showering together and then making long, slow love until they fell asleep in each other's arms.

Her smile wobbled, and she looked down, picking fruitlessly at the end of the packet.

'Here,' he said softly, and took it from her, finding the little red tab on the tear-strip and pulling it, opening the packet with ridiculous ease.

Their eyes met, and for an endless moment she thought he was going to kiss her, but then he put the biscuits down on the worktop beside her and went back to his coffee-making.

Her lungs unlocked and the breath eased out of her in a quiet sigh. So many memories—too many.

She never should have come here tonight.

CHAPTER FOUR

NICK stood in the middle of his empty study and sighed. He'd taken Sally home, and now he was back here alone, morosely drinking yet more coffee that he didn't need and which would doubtless keep him awake all night, and wondering how he was going to get through the next year or even longer working alongside her.

She just seemed so distant. Every time he got close to her she backed away. Every time he thought he'd made some progress, she put him down.

He couldn't blame her. Their relationship had left a lot of fall-out that she'd had to deal with alone, and it must have been unbelievably hard for her. He hadn't been able to think about anything but her and the baby since last night, and twenty-four hours later he was still coming to terms with a loss that was by definition remote, to say the least.

He couldn't understand why he was grieving for Amy, but he was. It was odd, and very unsettling. He looked around him one last time and headed for the spiral staircase. He was hungry, he was tired and he wanted to lie down somewhere comfortable and sleep for a week.

Not a chance—and tomorrow night he was on call and would have to sleep at the hospital, and the day after that his furniture was coming and he would have to start unpacking.

He went back to his temporary lodgings in the little motel just outside town and ate the take-away he'd picked up, while he listened to the television next door and the banging of doors up and down the corridor.

Much more of it and he'd go crazy, he thought. The sooner he was in his own house the better.

Nick looked tired again today, Sally thought as she went into the stores for more gauze and Steristrips. She wondered where he was staying until his furniture arrived. Funny, she'd assumed he would have rented somewhere for the duration of his time at the Audley, and the discovery that he'd bought a house just two miles away had thrown her a curve.

It implied some kind of long-term commitment to the area, but surely his post was only temporary? She did a quick mental calculation and realised this was probably his last rotation.

Which meant his next job would be a consultancy, wherever that turned out to be.

Here?

It was a possibility, she thought with a frisson of dread and excitement. In which case he'd be here for years.

Put him out of your mind, she told herself sternly. He's not your business any more. You don't need to think about him.

Right on cue he appeared in her line of sight and crooked a finger at her. So much for not thinking about him!

'I've got a problem,' he said in a low voice.

You and me both, she thought, only you're my

problem. 'How can I help you?' she asked, plastering on a bright smile.

His mouth tipped. 'That's a leading question,' he murmured, then in response to her quelling look his smile turned wry and he glanced over his shoulder at the cubicle he'd just vacated. She could hear a child wailing and the sounds of a sobbing woman.

'I've got a toddler I need to examine. He's yelling loud enough to bring the house down, she's not much better and I need someone to hold him still so I can get a look at his ears without inflicting permanent damage. Want to volunteer?'

'Sure. What's wrong with him? Otitis media?'

'That's my guess, but until I can get a look at his eardrums I can't be sure and he's not having any of it.'

She gave a little laugh. 'Sounds par for the course. Let's see what we can do.'

It took a minute or two, but eventually they managed to distract the toddler and reassure the mother. Then Sally had the baby on her lap with his head clamped firmly against her chest while Nick gently examined first one ear and then the other with the auriscope.

'OK. Give him back,' Nick mouthed. Well, in fact he might have said it, but Sally couldn't hear a thing for the screams of the protesting child.

Once back in his mother's arms, though, he settled to a steady wail and they could hear themselves think again.

'Well, as I thought, he's got a definite ear infection,' Nick told the worried mother. 'It's quite nasty, so I'm going to put him on antibiotics and a decon-

gestant for ten days, and you should give him para-
cetamol syrup every four hours to keep him comfortable. He'll soon be better, but if he doesn't improve
just take him back to see his GP. I'll give you a letter
for him.'

'There's no point. He refused to give him antibiotics for it. I've tried that. He says we should let nature take its course.'

A quick frown pleated Nick's brow. 'Was that recently?'

She shook her head. 'No. Last month. I thought he
was better, but then it started again and I thought, I
can't take him back to the GP, there's no point.'

'I think there probably is a point, if it's got worse,'
Nick explained thoughtfully. 'If the ear infection is
only slight, it can be better to let the body deal with
it and just use pain relief to keep the child comfortable. However, if it gets bad enough to make the child
really ill and distressed, you have to treat it or they
can suffer permanent damage. Maybe when you saw
your GP it wasn't severe enough to warrant it.'

She nodded a little doubtfully. 'I suppose you could
be right. It is worse now. I thought he was just being
callous.'

'I'm sure he wasn't.' He printed off the prescription, handed it to her with a note for the GP and sent
her off to the pharmacy with her little chap in tow
still wailing miserably.

'He really is unhappy, isn't he?' Sally said, listening to the wail retreating down the corridor. 'Was it
bad?'

'Pretty bad. The right ear was grim, the left was a
little red. My guess is he's had a cold and got bunged

up with catarrh and it just hasn't cleared. I've suggested to the GP that he might need referring if it happens again, but there was no obvious heat or tenderness in the mastoid process, so I think it's localised and the antibiotics and decongestant should sort it. Right, what's next? I'm parched.'

'Coffee?' Sally suggested, promptly kicking herself for falling for his hint, and he grinned.

'Sounds good. Is there any made?'

'Not to your satisfaction,' she told him drily. 'I tell you what, you go and put the pot on to filter, I'll see you in there in a minute. I've just got a dressing to finish off and I'll be with you.'

She went back to her patient, apologised for keeping him waiting and closed the wound in his forehead with the Steristrips, pulling the edges together neatly.

'There. Even your own mother wouldn't notice that after a few weeks,' she said in satisfaction, and grinned at him. 'Right, keep it dry, come back if you get any problems and you can take the strips off in a week if all goes well. And take it easy on the patio in future. No more falling over the geraniums!'

'Stone cold sober, as well,' he said with a wry grin. 'Ah, well. Thank you, Sister.'

'My pleasure. Mind how you go.'

She checked her watch. Almost eleven-thirty, and she'd been on since seven. More than time for a break, she thought, and sighed. She had a choice. Find something else to do and die of thirst, or go into the staffroom and expose herself to more of Nick's potent charm.

The thought of his coffee pushed her over the edge

and, shaking her head slowly at her own weakness, she took a deep breath and surrendered to temptation.

Nick was there, of course, lolling against the worktop chatting up one of her new nurses. The girl snapped to attention, put her mug down and left promptly, her guilty conscience showing a mile wide.

Sally didn't suffer a single twinge. She'd been wondering where the girl was for some time. Obviously she'd have to watch her—her attitude to breaks was apparently a little flexible.

'Coffee smells good,' she said brightly, and Nick chuckled.

He turned to her with a smile and held out a mug, gently steaming with fresh, fragrant coffee. 'Perfect timing,' he said, and his fingers brushed hers, sending heat shooting up her arm.

She nearly slopped the coffee. 'Thanks,' she murmured, and took the lid off the biscuit tin and sighed in disgust.

'Empty again,' she muttered. 'There's never a single biscuit by the time I get here.'

'Fancy one of these?' he asked, proffering an open packet of buttery oat biscuits. Her favourite sort.

She took one and bit into it with a groan of contentment. 'I love these,' she mumbled round the crumbs.

'I know. I remember.'

Her eyes flew up and clashed with his, and their gazes locked. Her heart lodged in her throat, hammering against her ribs and jamming the breath in her lungs. Was there nothing he didn't remember?

'I remember all sorts of things about you.' As if he could read her mind, he went on softly, his voice a caress, 'I remember your favourite shampoo, and the way you used to steal the quilt in the night and leave your slippers in the middle of the floor for me to fall over in the dark. I remember that you don't like broccoli and put tons of garlic in your spaghetti sauce, and you can't read while I'm driving because it makes you feel sick.'

She hardened herself against the soft, lyrical voice that was lulling her so dangerously. 'Do you also remember that I've managed without you for seven years, and that you didn't ring me when I needed you?' she retorted.

'You know damn well I didn't get the message,' he said tightly, and turned away, gripping the edge of the worktop. 'I tried, Sally—believe me, I tried. There was nothing else I could do. By the time I'd got the message, you'd just disappeared.'

'Morning, boys and girls! Is that your coffee, Nick? Smells good.'

'Morning, Ryan,' Sally said mechanically, and put her mug down on the worktop and headed for the door. 'Excuse me, both of you, but I have rather a lot to do.'

She fled from the staffroom and Nick's presence. It was more than she could cope with at the moment. *He* was more than she could cope with, and absolutely the last thing she needed to undermine her resolve was a trip down memory lane with him.

She focused her mind on the job by finding the junior nurse with the defective timekeeping and giving her a hard time about pulling her weight and not skiving off on unscheduled breaks. Then she softened the blow by taking her for a training session in suturing, when an elderly man came in with a neat slice in his leg from a sheet of broken glass.

'Right, it's a lovely clean cut, so I think, if Mr Brady doesn't mind, you can have a go,' she said after the initial instruction and the first couple of stitches.

'Not at all. I'm quite happy,' he said with a grin. 'Two beautiful women fussing over my half-naked body—it's enough to give me fantasies!'

'Just so long as it doesn't give you a heart attack,' Sally said with a teasing smile, and Mr Brady chuckled.

'I think I'm made of sterner stuff than that. You go ahead, my dears, I'll just lie here and enjoy the view.'

'A man of excellent taste.'

Sally looked up at the deep murmur and her eyes clashed with Nick's. 'There's a nasty fracture in the next cubicle waiting for you,' she said a little sharply, and turned her attention back to Sophie's stitching.

Mr Brady chuckled. 'Don't tell me, that's sexual harassment,' he said with a smile. 'How times change. I can remember the days when it was politically incorrect *not* to compliment your colleagues on their pretty looks.'

'What, even the male ones?' Sally teased, and he laughed and took her hand.

'You're a rum 'un,' he said with a twinkle. 'I reckon you'll make some lucky man a fine wife—or maybe you already have. Whatever, he's a lucky chap, whether he knows it yet or not.'

'Maybe I've got more sense,' Sally replied softly, easing her hand away. 'That's lovely, Sophie. Perfect. Not too tight—that's better. Well done. OK, Mr

Brady, we'll just dress that for you and you can go home. Stitches out in ten days if it looks well. You can have it done at your GP's, or come back to see us and we'll do it, or come sooner if they're sore or you have any problems. OK? And don't try to do too much—rest it up on a stool for part of the day, at least for the first few days.'

She sent him off with a note for his GP, and then she and Sophie cleared up the trolley and readied the cubicle for the next patient.

While they were doing it Sophie tipped her head on one side and gave Sally a searching look.

'Sister, don't you mind when they come on to you like that?' she said quietly.

'Are you talking about Mr Brady? I'd hardly call that coming on to me, Sophie. He was a charming man. You wait until you're on duty on Friday or Saturday night when the drunks get brought in by the police and they spend the entire time trying to get their hands up your skirt. Then tell me Mr Brady's a problem,' she advised drily.

Sophie's eyes widened. 'They do that?'

'They do all sorts. You learn to deal with it. You just keep as much distance as you can, stay polite if possible and call for help if you need to,' she said, patting the last pile of forms into order. 'Right, let's go and get on. With any luck it will be a young mother. They're usually pretty safe!'

'What are you doing for supper?'

Sally stiffened, refusing to jump like a startled rabbit yet again, and resolutely turned to face Nick.

'Nothing. Going home and examining the contents of my fridge,' she said firmly.

'Because I'm on call tonight and I've got to stay here, and I'm sick of eating alone.'

'So go and chat up one of the other nurses. I'm sure you'll find someone to fall for your charm and share some disgusting instant noodles in your room.'

He smiled a little crookedly. 'Maybe I don't want someone. Maybe I want you.'

'And maybe I don't want you,' she said crisply, hoping the lie didn't show in her eyes.

It didn't faze him at all. 'You could take pity on me,' he wheedled. 'I'll treat you. There's a little Italian round the corner, I've heard.'

He knew her too well. She could feel herself weakening and tried to drag some common sense into the argument. 'You won't get through the starter without your bleep going,' she warned.

'I'll risk it. Go on, Sally, force yourself. You never know, you might enjoy it.'

Sally hesitated, just long enough for him to see the chink in her armour and press his advantage.

'Just friends, Sal,' he coaxed, and he looked serious for a second. 'We have to work together. Surely we can manage that?'

She felt the fight go out of her, and gave him a wry smile. 'Just friends?'

That crooked grin which only a fool would have trusted played across his face. 'Absolutely. What time do you finish today?'

'Right now. I'm already late, as usual—and I'm going home to put on the washing machine and change into something that doesn't smell of hospitals. What time do you want me back here?'

He shrugged. 'Seven? Eight? I don't know. Whenever it's quiet.'

She snorted softly and shook her head. 'It's never quiet. You might do better to go to the canteen and find something there.'

'I'll risk it.' Nick reached up and touched the tip of her nose with his finger. 'I'll book a table for seven-thirty, shall I?'

'That's asking for trouble.'

'Very likely. I'll see you here at seven-fifteen.'

'All right,' she agreed, a little shiver of anticipation warring with her common sense.

She drove home to her little house, stripped off her clothes and threw them into the washing machine and then soaked in the bath.

It was bliss—or it would have been if she hadn't felt so edgy. Going to look at his house had felt like a date. What on earth would this feel like—and why on earth was she doing it?

Sally dressed carefully—much more carefully than the casual trousers and top deserved—and put on a lick of make-up. Not much, she never wore much, but just a touch. Something to hide behind.

It was nearly seven. She checked herself in the mirror, closed her eyes at her silliness and went out into the warm and pleasant evening. It was lovely, still light for hours yet, and she wondered why on earth she was going to sit with Nick in a stuffy restaurant and torture herself when she could be taking a stroll by the river or working on her slightly neglected garden.

Needless to say, Nick was busy, tied up with a patient Toby couldn't cope with alone. She waited in the staffroom, sipping old coffee, until he appeared at a quarter to eight.

'Sorry,' he said with a wry smile. 'You were right, of course. Shall we go?'

'Will we get away with it?'

His snort of laughter said it all. He took his wallet out of his locker and stuck it in his pocket, hung up his coat and pulled off his tie. 'Right, let's sneak out before this damn thing goes off,' he said, sliding his pager into his other pocket.

They drove, simply so that he could get back to the hospital quickly, and managed to park outside the little restaurant.

'Inside or out, sir?' the waiter asked, and Nick raised a questioning eyebrow at her.

'Out,' she said firmly. 'It's a lovely evening. It seems a shame to waste it.'

They had the last remaining table in the garden. It was getting cooler now and the sun would soon slide behind the houses, but for now the slanting rays bathed them in a gentle, golden light. The waiter offered them menus, but Nick didn't bother to look. 'I think we need something fairly quick, if you could,' he said with a persuasive smile. 'I might need to get back to the hospital if I'm paged.'

'No problem, sir. I could get you the house special in two minutes—tagliatelle carbonara?'

He looked at Sally, and she nodded. 'Lovely,' she said, her stomach gurgling slightly in appreciation, and she laid a hand over it and laughed. 'Sorry. I'm hungry.'

'Good.' He looked up at the waiter. 'That will be fine, thanks.'

'Garlic bread for you?'

His mouth kicked up and he caught her eye and smiled. 'Please.'

'And can I bring you the wine list?' the waiter asked, but Nick shook his head.

'I'm working, she's driving. Just iced water, please.'

'Very good, sir.'

He faded away, and left them. It was odd, Sally thought, how they could have been alone, even surrounded as they were by the crowd of laughing people at the other tables.

An awkward silence descended over them, and he smiled crookedly.

'I've missed you,' he said, and she felt her heart kick.

'Just friends, you said,' she reminded him, and his mouth quirked.

'I can miss my friends, can't I? Besides, you wouldn't want me to lie to you.'

'You'll have me believe you've been pining for me next,' she said drily, and a fleeting shadow crossed his face.

'Funny you should say that,' he said lightly, and sat back as the waiter put down their plates and left them again.

She didn't know how to answer him, so she picked up her fork and twirled it in the tagliatelle. Had he pined for her? Hardly, she thought. He was much too attractive to have been left alone, and only a fool or a saint could have failed to take advantage of some of those opportunities. In fact, she was surprised he hadn't been snared by some pretty young thing with buckets of sex appeal and too much sense to demand commitment.

'I would have thought you'd be married by now,' he said casually—too casually. She looked up and met his eyes, but they were carefully neutral.

'No,' she said. She didn't elaborate. There was no need. Nick had just reminded her of all the good reasons why she shouldn't be here with him—like the fact that he'd trashed the last seven years of her life and left her in an emotional wasteland.

'I nearly got married,' he said quietly, stopping her in her tracks, and she was astonished at the twist of pain she felt inside.

'Nearly?' she asked carefully.

'Yes—about three years ago. We were just jogging along, as you do, and it seemed like the next logical step. When she started talking about wedding plans, I realised it was a mistake.'

'Too much like commitment?' she said, a leaden feeling inside her that she couldn't understand. Had she hoped he'd changed? Not a chance. Leopards didn't change their spots, no matter how much you might want them to...

'Something like that,' he said lightly, but his eyes were giving nothing away as usual.

Oh, damn. Sally twirled pasta, munched garlic bread and wondered why the sun seemed to have gone in.

You're such a fool, she chastised herself. All that time you should have been getting over him, and you're just as weak-willed and defenceless against him as you ever were.

Because I still love him.

Idiot. Of course you don't. He's a disaster for you.

His bleep was almost a relief. He pulled it out of his pocket, stifled it quickly and read the message on the little screen.

'RTA coming in—just for a change. I need to get back.'

'I knew it,' she told him, struggling for a smile. 'You never get to finish a meal when you're on call in this place. A cup of coffee's hard to fit in without interruptions.'

'I had noticed.' He hailed the waiter, asked for the bill and looked apologetically at her. 'You stay and finish. I'll try and join you for coffee.'

'Get real,' she told him, and pushed away her plate. She wasn't hungry any more anyway. 'I'll come back with you—save me walking. I've been on my feet all day already.'

He paid the bill and they left, arriving back at the hospital as a fleet of ambulances started to pull up.

'Uh-oh,' Sally said under her breath. 'Looks like a lulu. Want a hand?'

'Try half a dozen,' he said, his mouth tight, then turned to her and gave her a little half-smile that didn't reach his eyes. 'We can manage if you want to get home.'

'I was thinking of the patients,' she told him, and followed him through the doors. 'I'll put scrubs on and see you in Resus.'

'You're a star,' he murmured, and followed her. 'Scrubs seem like a good idea.'

He stood beside her in the changing room and tugged off his shirt and trousers, standing next to her in nothing more than a pair of skimpy briefs and making her mouth go dry.

He'd bulked up, she realised, grown more solid over the years. Solid muscle, flexing under the smooth skin as he tugged on blue theatre pyjamas.

He shot her a glance and paused, balanced on one leg like a stork, half in and half out of the trousers. 'It's all yours,' he said softly under his breath. 'Just say the word.'

Released from her trance, she turned away and pulled off her blouse, dragging the top on over her head. 'In your dreams,' she muttered, but he'd gone, the door swishing softly shut behind him.

She sagged against the front of the lockers and sighed. Just friends, indeed! Not in this lifetime.

Anyway, there was no way she was going to let him tempt her into yet another transient affair. He'd just admitted to another failed relationship, another commitment he hadn't been able to make. She might be many things, but she wasn't a complete fool.

Just a little bit.

Like ninety-nine per cent.

With a disgusted snort at her weakness, she finished changing and headed for Resus.

It was a truly horrendous night. They fought to save the lives of three people—and twice, they lost. One man died of very serious head injuries soon after arrival, the other, a woman in her twenties, began to bleed internally on the way in and they couldn't transfuse her fast enough to get her stable.

They had three lines in, they were squeezing the bags of blood in flat out, but it still wasn't enough and a little after ten-thirty, she slipped away from them.

Nick ripped off his gloves, threw them in the bin in disgust and stalked out, slapping the door out of his way with the flat of his hand and striding down the corridor with a face like thunder.

Toby, still holding a bag of blood, looked after him warily.

'He's just angry with himself because we lost her,' Sally said gently, and took the bag out of Toby's hand. 'He'll be all right. He'll calm down in a minute.'

'I thought it was you that was supposed to have the temper?' Toby muttered under his breath, but she heard him and smiled.

'Oh, I have, too.'

'Dangerous place, then,' he said with a quick grin, and looked down at their patient, his smile fading. 'It seems such a waste.'

'I know.'

'Her parents are outside, apparently,' Meg, the staff nurse told them. 'Do you want me to clean her up? Take all the stuff off?'

Sally shook her head. 'No, it's all right, Meg. I'll do it. Someone needs to tell them. It really ought to be Nick.'

'Should I find him?' Toby asked, looking a little reluctant.

'He'll come back. He knows what he's got to do.' She stripped out all the IV lines and took out the tube in the young woman's throat, her hands as gentle as if her patient were still alive.

Poor girl, she thought. Toby was right, it was a terrible waste. She brushed the young woman's hair back off her bruised forehead with a hand that trembled slightly, and blinked away the tears.

She was getting soft in her old age. She needed distance, she reminded herself. It was a job, and to do it properly, she couldn't afford to allow herself to feel other people's pain.

Only sometimes, like this, it was impossible not to.

Her eyes swam with tears, and she blinked and Nick was there, his face carefully controlled.

'Is she ready for her parents?' he asked tightly, and Sally nodded.

'Yes.' She smoothed the soft, bruised skin again with a tender hand. 'Yes, she's ready. I'll come with you.'

Of all the jobs they had to do, this was the worst, she thought as they walked together up the corridor. There was no easy way to do it. She wondered how Nick would handle it, and knew instinctively that he would do it right.

The young woman's parents were in the interview room, and as Nick and Sally went in there, they stood up, shoulder to shoulder, as if they knew what was coming.

'Please, sit down,' Nick said gently, and they perched on the edge of the sofa, as taut as bowstrings. Their hands found each other and gripped, and Sally sat down next to the woman, offering silent support.

Nick sat down opposite her, turning towards them,

and now, for the first time, Sally saw the raw pain in his eyes.

He didn't prevaricate; there was no point. 'I'm sorry,' he said quietly. 'I'm afraid your daughter died a few minutes ago. We did everything we could, but her internal injuries were too severe and we weren't able to save her. I'm really sorry.'

Although Sally knew it was what they were expecting, his words extinguished the last spark of hope in the woman's eyes. 'No,' she whispered. 'Oh, no.'

Her husband held her, hanging onto her like a lifeline. After a moment he dragged in a deep, shaky breath. 'Can we see her?'

'Of course.'

They went down to Resus, and Sally had to blink away more tears as they made their tragic farewell.

'Did she suffer?' the mother asked in a strangled whisper.

'No. She was unconscious. She would have known nothing,' Nick assured them, and the woman slumped against her husband and shook her head numbly.

'We'll leave you alone with her for a moment,' Nick said, and drew Sally out and down the corridor into the stores. There he shut the door, pulled her gently into his arms and held her while she cried.

'I'm sorry,' she sniffed after a moment. 'It's just—'

'I know. It's such a waste. I know.'

She tipped her head back and saw the glitter of tears on his lashes, and knew that she would always love him, for this if for nothing else.

She knew they had no future. She knew she would get hurt again, but it didn't matter, because there would never be anyone else for her but him.

Friends or lovers, whatever, just as she knew the sun would rise in the east, she knew that he was her destiny, and nothing else mattered.

'Thank you,' she murmured softly, and, raising herself up on tiptoe, she touched her lips to his. Then she turned and went out into the corridor, back to Resus, to comfort the grieving parents of a girl whose destiny had come in the form of another car spinning out of control and cutting short her life.

Compared to that, the pain of loving Nick was a precious gift. She would cherish it in her heart, and relish every moment she had with him. It might have to last her a very long time.

CHAPTER FIVE

NICK went off duty at lunchtime the next day, feeling a little dazed from lack of sleep. The RTA Sally had helped with had been the start of a long and difficult night. Every time he'd tried to get his head down in the duty doctor's room, Toby had needed his help with another patient.

Finally at two o'clock, to avoid making Toby feel guilty every time he'd woken him, he'd just stayed up and worked alongside him, so that he'd been constantly available to give advice or assist with anything too demanding. In the end it had been just as well, because he'd walked into a cubicle to check a diagnosis just as Toby was about to inject a patient.

'I think it's heart failure or a pulmonary embolus. I've given her Lasix,' Toby said, checking a syringe. 'I'm just going to give potassium chloride to counteract the potassium loss.'

Nick crossed the room in a stride and put his hand on Toby's shoulder, squeezing it hard in warning. Strong potassium chloride injected intravenously from a syringe instead of slowly via a saline solution would have killed the patient instantly by stopping her heart. It was the method of choice for execution by lethal injection in the USA, because of its extraordinary effectiveness. Nick didn't want to find out firsthand just how effective it was, and he was darned sure Toby didn't either.

'You're giving it slowly, in saline, of course,' Nick said in a quietly authoritative voice that Toby couldn't fail to recognise.

His eyes widened, he looked down at the box containing the vials and blanched. 'Um—yes,' he said, a little breathlessly. 'Uh…'

Nick picked up the empty vial of Lasix and heaved a sigh of relief. The diuretic was just what she needed, judging by the way she was struggling for breath. Thank goodness he'd arrived in time to prevent the second injection.

'Why don't you put an IV line into her left hand while I just have a chat with our patient and find out a little history?' He moved to the head of the examination couch and bent over slightly, smiling at the oblivious patient propped up against the backrest and fighting for breath. 'Hello, there. Mrs Meadows, is it?'

'That's right,' the elderly woman gasped, holding the oxygen mask away from her face and nodding. 'Oh, I've got such a pain in my chest, and I can't breathe!'

'I know. Put the mask back on, I'll just have a listen to you. The drug you've been given should help to take some of the fluid off your lungs, and very soon you should feel better.'

He ran a stethoscope over her chest, front and back, and nodded. 'You've got a lot of fluid in there, and this should help, as I said, but I think we're going to need to have you in for a few days and look at you, just to make sure you're sorted and it doesn't happen again. Is there anyone we need to contact?'

'Oh, my daughter and my son, but they're a long way away.'

'I think we'll give them a ring and let them know you're poorly, and perhaps a neighbour could bring some things in for you tomorrow? In the meantime we'll just set up this drip and get you transferred to the medical admissions unit, and then the physicians can sort you out. OK?'

She nodded, and he noticed her breathing was already a little easier. He turned to Toby, still as white as a sheet and fumbling to put the line in.

'Um—her vein's a bit hard to find,' he said, but he hadn't even touched the skin, Nick noticed.

'I tell you what, why don't I take over from you and you can go and have a break for a few minutes? I'll see you in the staffroom when I've done this.'

Toby nodded slightly and fled, and Nick took over, locating the vein instantly and connecting up the saline drip with the potassium in it. A few minutes later Mrs Meadows, breathing easier, was transferred to the MAU and Nick went through to the staffroom and found Toby, white and shaking, his eyes red-rimmed with tiredness and tears.

'OK, let's go through this,' he said, sitting down and patting the chair beside him.

Toby perched on the edge of it, looking sick with fright, and Nick gave a grim smile. 'I'm not going to yell at you. I don't need to. You know damn well what you nearly did. What I want to know is why.'

Toby sagged back against the chair, his eyes haunted. 'I have no idea. I just—a mental glitch? I'm tired, I wasn't concentrating—I'll never do it again.'

'I know,' Nick said confidently. 'I'm absolutely

sure you'll never do it again. That's why I'm not going to report it, but we need to circumvent the possibility. You're too inexperienced to be hurled in at the deep end, and you need supervision. You need time to learn safely, and if you aren't absolutely sure, you have to ask, no matter how busy we all are, or you could end up with a tragedy. OK?'

Toby nodded, looking near to tears again, and Nick patted him on the shoulder. 'Go and kip for a while. Use my room. You're too tired to be of any help to the patients at the moment, so I'll take over. I'm up anyway.'

'Are you sure?'

'Absolutely. I've got the afternoon off tomorrow. You haven't. Go—sleep. I'll wake you if we have a crisis.'

He looked for Sally at seven, to have a quiet word with her about Toby, but she wasn't on duty until twelve. Odd, how the light seemed to go out of the day at that bit of news.

He told her about Toby when she came on duty, and she shook her head slowly.

'Oh, dear,' she said heavily. 'Was he mortified?'

'Just a touch. He's checking everything before he breathes now, but better to err on the safe side. I've spoken to Ryan, off the record, but I'm reluctant to make it official because I think Toby's got great potential and he's a good diagnostician. It's one of those stupid things we're all in danger of doing, and it's all part of the learning curve.'

'Hmm—and Toby's has just got steeper,' she said with a wry smile. 'Thanks for the warning. I'll keep an eye.'

To Nick's amazement it quietened down at one, so he went off a little early and arrived at his new house to find the furniture van outside, waiting to unload.

'Afternoon, guv,' the driver said, hopping down from the cab. 'All ready?'

He glanced at his watch, puzzled. 'Yes—I'm sorry, I've been at work. Have you been waiting long? I thought you'd be here at four.'

'We got away earlier than we thought, so we just came straight over. We've only been here long enough to eat our sandwiches. All right to unload now, or do you want us to hang on?'

He shook his head. The house had been left spotlessly clean, so it wasn't a problem that they were early. All they had to do was bring everything in and put it down in more or less the right place. 'Now will do fine. That's great. I'll just open up.'

He found the key and let them in, then remembered a clever idea he'd had in the middle of the night. 'I've drawn you a plan,' he said, fumbling in his pocket and pulling out a crumpled piece of paper. He smoothed it out on the hall wall, and jammed it under the light switch at the bottom of the stairs. 'There. That should help you find the rooms,' he said. 'What can I do to help?'

'Put the kettle on?' the driver's mate suggested, and Nick nodded again, a slight smile tugging at his lips as he remembered this crew from the pack-up of his old house last week.

Tea and biscuits—endlessly. He shot round to the supermarket conveniently sited a short distance away, stocked up on biscuits and cakes and more milk, and arrived back to find them wrestling a sofa into the sitting room.

'Tea and biscuits coming up,' he promised, and was rewarded with a grunt of approval.

They appeared just as he poured the milk into the mugs, and vacuumed up half a packet of biscuits before heading back to tackle the rest.

Redundant, since all boxes and possessions were clearly labelled to mark their destination, he found a suitcase with his old jeans in and started unpacking the books in his study and slotting them onto the shelves. He finished the last box as the removal men called up that they were finished, and within a few minutes they were on their way and he was alone in his house.

He cleared a space in front of one of the sofas and sat down, propped his bare feet on a box and looked around him in satisfaction.

It was wonderful. Complete and utter chaos, but wonderful.

Exhausted but content, Nick fell instantly asleep.

Oh, rats, Sally thought, her heart sinking. No car, and the lights weren't on. Nick must have gone back to wherever he'd been staying to pick up his things, or else to spend the night there. She was *sure*, though, that he'd said he was moving in this evening.

It was possible, of course, that he'd parked around the corner or popped out for a lightbulb or something silly like that.

Whatever, he just wasn't here—unless he'd already gone to bed, and that was unlikely.

Stifling the disappointment that she was reluctant

to acknowledge, she drove to the end of the little cul-de-sac beside his house to turn round, and blinked. His car was on the drive at the end of the garden, in front of a garage she hadn't realised was his.

So he was here, after all.

She parked beside the fence, removed the plant from the back seat and locked the car, then, screwing up her courage, she rang the bell.

For a minute nothing happened, then a light came on in the hall and the front door swung inwards to reveal Nick dressed in a scruffy, faded T-shirt and a pair of ancient and comfortable jeans. His feet were bare, his hair was tousled and spiky as if he'd been asleep, and his eyes were slightly unfocused. He blinked at her and stabbed a hand through the rumpled hair, doing nothing to improve it. 'Sally. Hi.' His voice was rough with sleep, and she felt a rush of guilt. He'd been on duty all night and, judging by the sound of it, it hadn't been easy.

'I'm sorry I woke you,' she said contritely, but he gave a wry laugh.

'It's OK. I just sat down for a minute—I must have dropped off. Busy night. Come in.'

He put his arm behind her, guiding her over the threshold, and she handed him the plant.

'A little bonsai tree for your study—I know you love trees and it seemed appropriate in your tree-house. Don't forget to water it every day, though.'

He looked a little choked for a second, then gave her a crooked smile. 'Thank you.' He bent to kiss her, his lips making fleeting contact before he straightened and stepped away. 'Come on in. Let me get you a

drink. I've got a bottle of fizzy that's been in the
fridge for a few hours—want to crack it with me?'

'I'm driving,' she reminded him, a little reluctantly.

'You could stay for a while,' he suggested. 'Let it
wear off. I could order a pizza or Chinese or something to go with it.'

He gave her one of his persuasive little grins, and
she shook her head in despair. She'd already eaten,
but only toast in the staffroom at six, and it was
tempting.

'You seem to spend your life feeding me these
days,' she protested weakly.

'You could help me unpack boxes,' he suggested,
'if you feel you need to earn the meal.' His words
were innocent enough, but his eyes twinkled, and she
was lost.

'I knew there was a catch,' she said with a laugh.

He stifled the smile, and one brow quirked in enquiry. 'Well?'

'OK—just a little glass, just this once as you're
celebrating, and I'll let you feed me if you insist,' she
relented, disgusted with herself for crumbling so easily and yet only too willing to be talked into it. 'And
we'll unpack some of your things.'

Nick's grin widened, crinkling the corners of his
eyes and bringing his face alive, and she thought how
good he looked, how dear and familiar and just down-
right gorgeous, with his chin roughened by the day's
growth of beard and his hair all untidy and his eyes
smiling like that.

Gorgeous and utterly dangerous, except that she
was already addicted so it didn't really matter. Sally
smiled back.

'So where is it, then, or was that just an empty threat?'

He chuckled and pulled the bottle out of the fridge. 'Here's the champagne. Goodness knows where the glasses are.'

'Use mugs,' she said pragmatically.

He looked shocked. 'It's a Möet!' he said, scandalised.

Sally just laughed. 'Don't be pompous,' she told him, and started ferreting about in the boxes. 'Here—this one says glasses. Shall I unpack it, if you're going to be precious?'

He snorted rudely and went up to the study, coming back a moment later with the telephone directory. 'Chinese, Indian or pizza?'

'Indian. Chicken korma and plain rice, a chapati and mango chutney, please.'

'Such a creature of habit,' he murmured, and ran his finger down the list of numbers.

'The Taj Mahal is the best,' she told him. 'Cheap, quick and yummy—and they deliver.'

He nodded, scanned the list again and punched in a number on the wall phone by the fridge.

'I bet you have a jalfrezi and pilau rice,' she murmured, just as he started to order it.

He rolled against the wall, turning to look at her while he spoke, his mouth twitching into a grin as he did exactly as she'd said.

'"You're such a creature of habit!"' she mimicked, and he gave the address, hung up and laughed softly.

'So we're as bad as each other,' he said. 'Found those glasses yet?'

'I've found something vaguely wineglass-ish. Not flutes.'

'They'll do.' Nick threw her a new teatowel, and she gave them a rinse, wiped them with the ineffectual cloth and put them on the worktop just as he popped the cork. The champagne foamed into the glasses, and he ceremoniously handed her one.

'To your house,' she said, raising the glass, and he clinked it with his.

'To—the house,' he said softly, their eyes locked, and he lifted the glass to his lips and drank.

There had been an infinitesimal pause before he'd changed her wording. Why? Surely he hadn't been about to say 'our house', had he? Oh, Lord. And the way he was looking at her...

To cover her confusion Sally took a gulp of the wine, but the bubbles tickled her nose, and she wrinkled it and laughed, breaking the tension of the moment. 'So—unpacking,' she said, a little breathlessly, and he seemed to take a second to focus on her words.

'Yes—um, plates would be good. I bought their dishwasher. I think everything could do with going through it to get the newsprint off, but we'll need a couple of plates to eat off in the meantime. I think they're in here.'

He put his glass down and crouched by a box, slitting the tape with his keys and opening it. It was the right one, so between them they unpacked it and loaded the dishwasher. While he tackled the next box, Sally washed two of the plates and then spent a few fruitless minutes trying to find cutlery.

'Ah, that's in my spaghetti jar to stop it crashing

about,' he said, brandishing it, and she rolled her eyes and laughed.

'Obvious, really. The first place I would have thought of looking.'

'Of course. Where else?' He reached into the jar and pulled out a bundle of cutlery. 'Hey pasto!' he said with a grin, and whether because of the champagne or the silliness of the joke or just sheer enjoyment of each other's company, they started to laugh, and once they'd started, they couldn't stop.

It was one of those crazy sessions that left them leaning against the worktop wheezing and sighing, wiping their eyes and still chuckling minutes later, but then he reached out a hand and touched her cheek, and the laughter faded, replaced by a breathless tension.

'You're still beautiful, do you know that?' he murmured, and she felt the heat of his touch right down to her toes.

Oh, Lord, he's going to kiss me, she thought. Really kiss me, and then what will happen, because I can't deny him anything—?

The doorbell rang, and his mouth kicked up in a crooked smile. 'Supper,' he murmured, and went out to the hall, giving her a moment to collect herself.

Her heart thumped against her ribs, and she busied herself clearing a space on the worktop for the takeaway so she didn't have to meet his eyes. Had she totally misread his intentions? Maybe she'd imagined the tension between them—

'Here we go.' Nick dumped the bag on the space she'd cleared, pulled out the little cartons and they dished up and took their plates and glasses through to the sitting room.

'It's not exactly tidy, I'm afraid, but the dining room's even worse,' he told her, clearing a space on one of the two-seater sofas. To her relief he sat on the other one at right angles to her, still close but with that little bit of space so she could breathe without touching him.

Silly, really, when all she wanted to do was touch him, but that would be so foolish and, destiny or not, she had to work with him. Anyway, she wasn't even sure it was what he wanted. He'd said something only last night about being friends. Maybe he really meant it. He'd also said he was all hers, when he'd been changing, so what he really meant was anybody's guess.

'OK?' he asked, and she nodded. Sally didn't know what he was talking about—the food? Probably. She couldn't really taste it. She was too busy wondering what would have happened if the delivery man hadn't chosen that exact moment to ring the bell, and if she'd really misread him when once she'd known his every thought.

He topped up her glass, and she sipped the champagne and thought about driving home, and put it down again. 'I don't suppose I could be boring and have a glass of water, could I?' she said, and he shot her a crooked grin and went out to the kitchen to fetch it.

'I don't know, some people just won't be led astray,' he murmured, putting it down beside her on a box, and she arched a brow.

'Led astray?' she said, her heart thumping. She

tried for a light-hearted, teasing tone. 'Are you trying to get me drunk and seduce me?'

'As if I would do a thing like that,' he said innocently.

She gave a rude snort, and his mouth lifted into a wry smile.

'I suppose I was hoping you might stay a little longer.'

'Might have to, you mean,' she said drily. 'The choice would be nice.'

His smile faded. He sighed and rammed a hand through his short, spiky hair, rumpling it even more, and met her eyes, his own resigned. 'It's your choice, Sally. If I can find the coffee-maker, I'll put some coffee on in a minute. It's up to you if you stay long enough to have it, or go now. Hell, you can stay the night if you like. There are plenty of places to sleep. I'm not going to force you to do anything.'

Since when did force come into it? He only had to look at her and she was lost!

'I don't think I'll be staying the night,' she said softly, and he laughed, a short, humourless huff of sound that was curiously painful.

'I didn't think for a moment that you would. I'll make the coffee.'

Nick stood up and went out, leaving his meal unfinished, and she picked around in her rice and ate the chicken and felt guilty. She shouldn't have come, really. She should have left him alone, instead of coming round here and throwing herself at him and then playing the affronted virgin.

He *had* said he wanted to be friends, and maybe he'd really meant it. Perhaps the crack about being all hers had been exactly that. Besides, absolutely the last thing she wanted was to get involved with him again in a physical relationship that was destined to go nowhere.

And a relationship with a man who didn't do commitment was a recipe for disaster as far as she was concerned. Sally put her plate down and stood up, just as he came back into the room.

'I think I'll go,' she said quietly. 'It wasn't a good idea, coming here, for either of us, and I'm just keeping you up. You need some sleep.'

'I have to find sheets first,' he said, his eyes scanning her face. 'Sally, stay for a while. I'm sorry I gave you the champagne, I really didn't have an ulterior motive. I wasn't really thinking.'

She believed him. He'd never lied to her.

'Anyway,' he went on, that coaxing, wheedling tone back in his voice, 'you did say you were going to help me with the unpacking, and I really do have to find sheets and towels and things like that before I can sleep. You couldn't leave me here exhausted and in such a muddle, could you?'

She laughed despite herself. 'Now you really are piling it on too thick,' she said drily. 'The day you're that helpless will be a cold day in hell.'

A flash of humour lit his eyes. 'You know me too well,' he said ruefully, and sat down on the sofa again and picked up his plate. 'You haven't finished,' he pointed out, and her motives for leaving suddenly seemed very blurred and uncertain.

'So I haven't,' she murmured, and she sat down again. There was no point in wasting it when she really was hungry.

'So, tell me where you've been until now,' she said when they'd finished and were settled down again with a cup of coffee.

'Oh, just about everywhere in the area,' he told her, and detailed all the posts he'd had and who he'd worked with. Some of the names were familiar from their own department, not necessarily people she'd worked with but others who'd been there in the past and moved on. It seemed odd that it hadn't worked the other way, and that none of the people coming to them might have known of him or mentioned him, but they hadn't, or she would have known he was about. Still, people didn't tend to talk about past colleagues very much.

'So why East Anglia?' she asked.

After a moment he shrugged, studying his coffee-mug in minute detail. 'I had to work somewhere. It's got some fine hospitals and some lovely countryside, it's near London in case I need a cultural fix—why not?'

Nick met her eyes, his own bland and unreadable. He was hiding something, but she'd only get herself in trouble if she tried to work out what. Something to do with his ex, or another woman? Sally let it go for now and put her mug down.

'Right, unpacking. We need to find you sheets so you can get to bed,' she said briskly, standing up, and with a mild grumble about being harassed, he got to his feet and followed her out to the kitchen, dumping their dishes in the sink.

'It's a mess,' he warned her as they went upstairs. 'There's no way we can find the bed tonight.'

That might be just as well, she thought wryly to

herself, if her body was going to continue to react to his like this! They went into the main bedroom and she stopped dead and stared at it in dismay. A mess? That didn't even begin to touch it!

'If it's not a rude question, just where did you intend to sleep?' she asked mildly, and he laughed.

'I'll find a square inch. I need to get the mattress down flat—if you can help me shift things enough to do that, and find some sheets and my quilt and pillows, I'll be a happy man.'

'Why on earth didn't you stay where you were for one more night?' she asked, randomly grabbing a box and stacking it out of the way.

His derisive snort said it all. 'I'd had enough of other people's televisions and doors banging and footsteps overhead and general coming and going all night—it was hell, and to cap it all there was a gap under the door that let the light in from the corridor. I couldn't get out of there fast enough.'

She could imagine. Nick had always hated noise at night, and the slightest chink of light would keep him awake. Most doctors had trained themselves to sleep standing up in the middle of a party, but Nick was obviously not one of them.

'Any idea where the sheets and stuff might be, before we bury them with a load of other boxes?'

'Not really. Everything's labelled,' he told her. 'Just look at the boxes.'

'Would "airing cupboard" cover it?' she asked after a moment's searching.

'Sounds about right.'

'Here's a possible, then.' Sally dragged the box

away from the wall, but the corner of another box was resting on it and the pile teetered wildly.

'Careful!' he warned, leaning across her to stop them falling, and his chest brushed her arm. Heat shot up it, and she had to stifle the urge to lean against him.

Friends, she reminded herself, just friends, and ducked out from under his arm while he straightened the stack. Five minutes later the floor was clear and the mattress was down.

Nick put his hands on his hips and grinned tiredly. 'Right, all we need is a bottom sheet, the quilt and my pillow on there and I can lie down. Bliss.'

She shook out the sheet, and together they knelt down on each side of the mattress and tucked it in, then Sally sat back on her heels and looked across at him. There was a curiously intense expression on his face, and if she hadn't known better—

She got hastily to her feet, brushing off the knees of her jeans so she didn't have to meet those strangely expressionless, burning eyes. 'Right, you can manage now, can't you?'

It seemed to break the spell. He stood up, grabbed the pillow and lobbed it at the head of the bed, then shot her a crooked grin. 'Yes, I can manage,' he said drily. 'Thank you.'

'My pleasure. Sleep well. I'm sure you will.'

'I'm sure I will—if the silence doesn't keep me awake!'

He followed her down the stairs, and she paused at the front door and thanked him for the meal, and he looked down at her with that unreadable expression in his eyes and smiled a tiny, twisted little smile.

'Thank *you*, Sally,' he murmured. 'Thank you for everything.' His hand came up and cupped her cheek, and his lips grazed hers lightly before he released her and opened the door.

'I'll see you on Monday,' he said, 'unless you feel the unaccountable urge to help me unpack over the weekend?'

Sally laughed, a little breathlessly. 'Not a chance, buster. You're on your own for that one,' she retorted. 'There's only one thing I hate more than moving out, and that's moving in. If you don't unpack your stuff, you'll never find anything.'

'It might be worth the risk,' he murmured with a slight smile, and she had the sudden distinct feeling that he was lonely.

Nick Baker, lonely?

Not a chance.

But he was still watching her, his hand raised in farewell, as she turned the corner in her car...

CHAPTER SIX

SALLY'S conscience prickled her all through Saturday, while she cleaned her house and waged war on the garden and hung out her washing. Not that it needed to, because she was hardly lolling about sunbathing or anything while Nick was working his fingers to the bone, but she couldn't get rid of the nagging thought that he was lonely and unhappy.

She tried to tell herself that he deserved it, but her heart wasn't listening to her head, and first thing Sunday morning she got up, made a lemon drizzle cake and drove round to his house.

He was in the garden, and he saw her over the fence as she parked on the other side of it. 'Hi,' he said, smiling and folding his arms along the top. 'Couldn't stay away, I see.'

She stifled the urge to throw the cake at him. It would be such a waste. 'I've brought you a present.'

'Another one!' he said, surprised.

'Only a cake,' she told him crushingly. 'Have you watered my tiny tree yet, by the way, or have you killed it already?'

'Of course I've watered it. Poor little thing, it hasn't got any roots. It needs regular drinks.'

'Just don't feel sorry for it and plant it out in the garden,' she advised, and he chuckled.

'Don't worry, I won't. Are you coming in, or would that involve an unconscionable loss of face?'

'I'm coming in,' she said drily. 'If that's all right?'

'Sure. Here, come through the gate.'

She squeezed past his car and went through the gate he was holding open, and handed him the cake— or tried to. His fingers were dirty, and he held them up in protest.

'Are you weeding?' she asked, looking around.

'Just planted a house-warming present.'

How absurd, to feel a pang of jealousy! Other people were allowed to give him presents.

'It's from me,' he said, as if he could read her mind. 'It's a Japanese maple—*Acer palmatum dissectum atropurpureum.*'

'Are you trying to impress me?' she said drily, and he laughed.

'Does it work?'

She shook her head, and he laughed again. 'It's an old friend, actually. It was in my last garden. I've had it in a pot since the spring, because I knew I was moving. I thought it ought to go back out into the garden, so I'm watering it copiously. It's over here— come and say hello.'

'Tree-hugger,' she muttered, hiding her smile, and followed him over to a little arching plant, more shrub than tree in size, its leaves deeply cut and a wonderful dark purplish bronze.

'Isn't she lovely?'

'She? It'll have a name next.'

'Don't get picky,' he told her with a grin. 'Come in, I've just put a pot of coffee on. I must have known you were coming.'

'You'll OD on the stuff one day,' she warned, fol-

lowing him inside, then she stopped in her tracks.
'Oh, wow! You've put everything away.'

'There wasn't that much, and I've got plenty of
cupboards.'

'So you didn't need my help at all,' she said accusingly, and he grinned.

'This is just the kitchen,' he reminded her. 'I'm
sure I can find something useful for you to do else-
where—if you've had a change of heart.'

She humphed and looked in the cupboards for
plates and mugs.

'This what you're looking for?' he asked, taking a
couple of plates from what seemed like a totally ar-
bitrary cupboard.

She glanced over her shoulder and straightened,
frowning. 'Yes—what an odd place to put them!'

'You had your chance for a say,' he pointed out
fairly, and she coloured and shut up. She didn't need
to be familiar with his kitchen. It was up to him where
he put his blasted plates.

'Milk or cream?'

'Cream? Good grief,' she said weakly. 'Are we being a little self-indulgent?'

He gave one of his sassy, little-boy grins that
flipped her heart. 'Yes, we darned well are! So, which
is it to be?'

'Oh, cream, every time,' she said with a laugh.
'The cake should still be warm, by the way.'

'I know, I felt it. I have designs on it, don't worry.
Let's go in the garden.'

They carried their mugs and plates outside, and sat
down near the little Japanese tree and listened to the

dribbling of water and the whisper of leaves and the playing of children in the distance.

'It's so peaceful,' she said enviously. 'My garden's surrounded by noisy teenagers.'

He shuddered eloquently and bit into his cake. 'Revolting,' he muttered.

'The cake?'

'The teenagers.' His grin was infectious, and she found herself relaxing. He was good company. He always had been. That was what had drawn them to each other—that and the amazing sensuality that seemed to sizzle between them.

It was sizzling now, in a very low-key way, just a companionable attraction reflected in the way their eyes met and held. 'I've missed you,' he said quietly after a moment. 'Missed your friendship. Missed your sense of humour.'

'Missed my temper?'

He pulled a doubtful face. 'Not much evidence of it in the last week. Everyone talks about it, but I haven't seen more than the odd trace.'

'That's because you haven't annoyed me enough yet.'

'Good grief. It never used to take me so long, I must be losing my touch.' He smiled, and she felt herself soften.

Oh, Nick, she thought. We lost so much...

He looked down into his mug, his face thoughtful. He was debating something, she could tell, but she had no idea what.

'Penny for them.'

He shook his head. 'No. It doesn't matter.'

'What? Come on, you always used to be able to ask me or tell me anything.'

After a moment he met her eyes, and his were troubled. 'It's about Amy.'

Sally's heart thumped, and as casually as she could manage she leant back against the chair for support. 'What about her?'

His shoulders lifted a fraction in a tiny shrug. 'I hate bringing it up, because I don't want to hurt you and I don't know if I have the right to ask, but—there are things I want to know.'

'It's OK,' she told him, and realised that it was. There were things she wanted him to know—things she wanted to show him. She leant forwards. 'Ask away.'

He paused, then said carefully, 'I just wondered— what happened to her? After she died? Was there a funeral? I suppose there must have been. Was she christened?'

'Yes, she was christened, by the hospital chaplain. She's buried in the churchyard of the village where I grew up,' she told him gently. 'My parents were still living there then, but my grandmother's had a stroke so they've moved to Devon now. It's only a few miles away. I'll show you, if you like.'

His face looked strained. 'Would you? It would help to make it real.'

'Sure. When do you want to go? We could go now, if you like. It only takes half an hour to get there.'

'Not now,' he said, glancing at his watch. 'It's Sunday morning, the church will be heaving.'

She shook her head. 'No. It's a united benefice. The services rotate between the local churches—and anyway, it won't be heaving, exactly, even in full swing. It's only a tiny village.'

He nodded. 'OK, then. If it's quiet. I just want a little privacy.'

She gave him a reassuring smile. 'It's OK, I understand. Shall we go?'

'Do you mind?'

'No. Of course I don't. I often go to see her.'

A fleeting pain crossed his face, and she wondered if she'd done him a huge disservice by not contacting him about her. She really hadn't thought he'd care, and yet he obviously did.

Had she really been so wrong about him?

They went in his car. When they arrived the church car park beside the village hall was deserted. She led him along the paths and then over the lush, soft grass to a row of little headstones. There, weathering slightly now, was a simple white marble stone, engraved with the baby's name and the date.

Only one date, of course, because she'd only had that one short day.

'There,' she said, pointing to it.

'You gave her my name,' he said, his voice strangled. Crouching down, he ran a hand lightly over the words, and then it trailed down to rest flat on the grass in front of the stone, over where she lay.

Sally was unaware of the tears on her cheeks. She knew only that he was grieving, and that this was something she should have done years ago.

After a while he stood up and turned away, his face ravaged with tears, and she blew the headstone a little kiss and followed him.

'Nick?'

He stopped, and she turned him into her arms and held him. A shudder ran through him, and his arms came up round her and hugged her close, rocking her gently against his chest.

They stood like that for ages, then finally she eased away and looked up at him.

'Are you OK?' she asked, and he nodded, his face sombre.

'Yes, I'm OK. I'm sorry. I didn't think it would hit me that hard. What about you? Are you all right?'

She nodded. 'I'm fine. Are you OK to drive?'

His smile was gentle and a little sad. 'I'll do. Come on, let's go home.'

It sounded wonderful. What a shame it was just a figure of speech.

They pulled up outside his house and he let them in, then turned and drew her into his arms. 'Thank you for taking me,' he said gruffly.

'That's all right,' she murmured and, lifting a hand, she cradled it gently against his cheek.

Their eyes locked. For an age time seemed suspended, then after an endless pause he turned his head and touched his lips to her palm.

Out of nowhere heat flared between them, and his hands came up, tunnelling through her hair and cupping her head, steadying it against the desperate onslaught of his mouth. She was starving for him, aching for him, and her arms locked around him and held him closer.

He shifted, turning her against the wall so his leg meshed between hers and his body was crushed against her. A groan rocked through him, and suddenly she didn't care about common sense. She didn't care about anything except Nick, and being closer to him, much closer, so close she couldn't tell where he ended and she began.

They belonged together, like this, and nothing else mattered.

'Sally?' he whispered raggedly, and she eased away, taking his hand in hers and leading him upstairs.

The bedroom was still in chaos, the mattress on the bed now but the quilt thrown off onto the floor. It didn't matter. They didn't need the quilt.

Just each other.

Lifting her in his arms, Nick lowered her to the bed and came down beside her, his body half over hers, his mouth finding hers again hungrily.

Her fevered fingers plucked at his clothes, but he covered her hands and paused. 'Are you on the Pill?' he asked, and she stared at him, stunned. Had she totally lost her mind? The *last* thing she needed was another unplanned pregnancy!

'Oh, damn,' she said, furious with fate for snatching away this opportunity, but he smiled and put a finger on her lips.

'It's OK. I've got something.'

He looked round the room, and she gave a hollow, despairing laugh.

'Don't tell me, they're in a box somewhere.'

He grinned and shook his head, then hung over the side of the mattress, his voice muffled. 'No. I bought them the other day. Here. I put them under the bed.'

He came up with a pharmacy bag and dropped it on the mattress beside her, and she felt her desire drain away. She stared at it distrustfully, a cold feeling spreading over her. 'Did you plan this?' she asked, very, very quietly, and he groaned and dropped onto his back beside her, one arm flung up over his face.

'No, Sally, I didn't *plan* it.'

'Are you sure? It looks pretty planned to me.'

He moved his arm and met her eyes. For once she could read his expression, and in it she saw frustration and disappointment. 'Yes, I'm sure,' he said with studied emphasis. 'I didn't plan it—not as such. I just thought, if there was the slightest chance—I didn't want to make any more mistakes, Sally. I've done you enough damage.'

She sat up and wrapped her arms around her legs, feeling suddenly unsure of everything—of him, of her, of what they were about to do.

'Sally?'

She looked back down at him over her shoulder, and his eyes were filled with understanding. 'It's your choice,' he said softly. 'I'm not going to put any pressure on you. It's entirely up to you.'

She stared at the bag, looking for an answer, but she knew what it would be. Sadly, reluctantly, she slid to the edge of the bed and stood up.

'I'm sorry,' she said, her voice quiet and defeated. 'I don't think I'm ready for this. Maybe I never will be.'

He closed his eyes—counting to ten? Then he jack-knifed off the edge of the bed.

'Forget it, it was a lousy idea anyway. They always say you should never go back.' He headed for the door, pausing to hold it for her. She went past him and down the stairs, and at the bottom she hesitated only long enough to pick up her bag.

'I'll see you tomorrow,' she said, and he grunted something unintelligible and opened the door. As she walked down the path towards her car, she heard the door close with a decisive click, and she could have cried with frustration.

She was doing the right thing, the sensible thing, but she wanted to be in there with him, not out here, going home alone.

Nick went back up to the bedroom, grabbed the little white paper bag off the bed and hurled it with all his strength into the corner of the room. It hit the wall harmlessly and dropped down behind a pile of boxes, and he left it there. It didn't matter if he never found it again. He wasn't going to have a use for the contents, and he was all finished being a good boy scout.

He sat down abruptly on the edge of the bed and gave a harsh sigh. He was behaving like a toddler who'd had his favourite toy taken away, and for two pins he'd throw himself down on the floor and drum his feet in frustration.

'Oh, Sally,' he sighed, and shook his head slowly from side to side. 'I'm such an idiot. Why didn't I think about how you'd react?'

Because he hadn't planned it, quite genuinely, was the answer. If he had, he would have had a condom in every part of the house and in his car, his wallet, the pocket of his white coat—anywhere, just to be on the safe side. Instead he'd messed up, and it had given her time to think.

Better than regretting it later, he reminded himself,

and with one last longing glance at the bed, he went downstairs, put their coffee-mugs and cake plates in the dishwasher and put the rest of the cake in the fridge. He'd take it to work tomorrow—no doubt they'd manage to eat it between them.

Then he went back out into the garden, belatedly turned off the hose that was watering in the little Japanese maple, and set about unpacking and sorting out the garden tools and equipment.

By the following morning all that was left of Nick's frustration was a lingering regret. He'd had time to analyse the situation, and one thing became clear. The only reason they'd gone upstairs to bed had been because of Amy, because they'd been seeking comfort from each other, and that was a lousy reason to restart an old affair.

He'd suggested friendship as a cover, initially. Now he began to think it might be a genuinely good idea—always supposing that Sally still wanted to be friends with him after yesterday.

He parked his car, strode through the hospital and hung up his jacket, retrieving a new white coat and swapping the things in the pockets. Friendship, he told himself firmly. That was the way to go. He'd talk to her, just as soon as he could get her alone for long enough.

It was one of those Mondays where everybody had sat on their symptoms all weekend, phoned the GP and been told they couldn't have an appointment until Tuesday week, so they'd all trotted down to A and E

to have their ears syringed and their tonsillitis diag-
nosed and their ingrowing toenails inspected.

Sally spent the morning educating—not only the
public, who needed a better understanding of what
constituted an accident or an emergency, but the
young nurses who were new in the department.

Training was a large part of her job, and often she
didn't have time to do it properly. Now she trained,
supervising them as they undertook routine jobs in
the department—putting on new plaster casts, removing stitches, suturing simple wounds and so on.

It was a part of her job that she enjoyed, but she
wasn't in the best mood and frankly a good old pile-
up on the dual carriageway would have been welcome
to take her mind off Nick.

She was painfully aware of him prowling around
the department. Every time she stuck her head out of
a cubicle he seemed to be there, and it was doing
nothing for her peace of mind.

Why on earth, she kept asking herself, had she
walked away? She should have stayed. Premeditated
or not, it was better than being caught unawares and
getting pregnant again, and it was hardly as if she had
been an unwilling victim!

She sighed heavily and dropped the notes back into
the slot outside the cubicle while the X-ray result was
awaited, and turned to find Nick there, just inches
away.

'Sally,' he said softly, and her heart melted.

Oh, you fool, she chastised herself. You could have
been with him last night.

'Time for a coffee?'

She dithered, but he cranked up the wattage of his

smile and she was lost. 'OK, just a quick one while we wait for that X-ray result.'

There was nobody in the staffroom, and he closed the door behind them to give them privacy.

'About yesterday,' he said without preamble.

Her heart skittered. 'Not here, Nick. Not now.'

'Where, then? My place? Yours? How about dinner? We need to talk, Sally.'

'I know.' She worried her lip and thought for a moment. 'What about lunchtime?'

'It never works,' he pointed out fairly, 'and we need to have this talk. There are things I want to say to you—things I need to say.'

He sounded so serious. She began to feel edgy, worried. What could he be going to say? Nothing that should feel even remotely like a threat, she told herself, and yet she felt a shiver of dread. Absurd, since she had nothing to lose. Unless—surely he wasn't going to offer her a commitment? Her heart thumped again, and she swallowed.

'Tonight?' she suggested. Whatever he wanted to say to her, privacy would be a good thing, and she didn't fancy being stuck in a pub or restaurant—or driving afterwards, come to that. 'Why don't you come to me?' she went on. 'I could cook for us.'

'OK. What time?'

She shrugged, running a mental eye over the contents of her freezer and coming up with nothing. 'Seven-thirty?' That should give her time to shop, cook and get ready for whatever it was he had in mind.

'Seven-thirty's fine. How about coffee?'

She realised distractedly that Nick was talking

about now, waving the pot at her, his eyebrows arched in enquiry.

'Thanks.'

He handed her a mug, and just as she was wondering how on earth she could get through five minutes of small talk with their scheduled 'chat' hanging over her, a tall, fair man strolled in, dropped a friendly arm around her shoulders and smiled at Nick, extending his hand.

'You must be Nick Baker. Matt Jordan—it's a pleasure to meet you.'

Sally smiled up at him, only too glad of the diversion. 'How was your holiday?' she asked when the introductions were complete. 'Had a good time in Canada?'

He nodded, his smile widening. 'Amazing. Sarah loves it over there, and my parents were thrilled to see their grandchildren again. It was just wonderful, but I think I OD'd on family! So, how are things here?'

'Oh, you know—this morning they don't understand the difference between A and E and their GP surgeries.'

He groaned. 'That again. Still, it's better than the other thing.'

Just then Nick's bleep sounded, and with a wry laugh he set down his mug and headed for the door.

Matt watched him go, then his glance flicked back to Sally. 'Seems a nice enough guy. What kind of doctor is he?'

'A perfectionist,' she said without hesitation, and Matt grinned.

'Excellent. We could use a few more of them. How's our new SHO shaping up?'

'Ah. Less of a perfectionist. He made a potentially nasty boob the other day. I don't know what Nick said to him, but now he asks before he blows his nose. Nick thinks he's going to be a good doctor, though.'

Matt rolled his eyes. 'Great. A babysitting job. I can hardly wait to meet him.' He sniffed experimentally. 'That coffee smells good.'

'It is. Nick made it, he's dead fussy. I have to leave you to it, Matt. Come and find me, I'll fill you in on the news later.'

'OK.'

She went back to her list of malingerers, and found the X-ray result that she'd been waiting for was back.

'Want me to have a look?' Ryan said, appearing behind her shoulder.

'Please, if you would. It's Toby's patient.'

'I know.' He snapped the film up on the light box at the work station, and pursed his lips. 'OK. Let's call Toby. This is quite a tricky fracture to spot—I'd like to see if he can find it.'

Toby was busy suturing a nasty tear, but Sally called Meg, who was free to take over the suturing, and Ryan and Toby studied the film while Sally waited.

'It's fractured,' Toby said cautiously. 'There, across the waist of the scaphoid.'

'Are you sure?' Ryan asked.

Toby looked again. 'Yes, I'm sure. It's very hard to see, but I'm pretty certain.'

'How would you be sure?'

'Another view? A repeat of this one, perhaps, in a

few more days? It might not show up for ten days or so, but the symptoms fit and I'd be inclined to plaster it anyway for a few days and then check it, even if I couldn't see anything. She's got tenderness in the space between the thumb and first finger, a weak pinch, it hurts on hyperextension—and I can see it anyway, I'm sure, even though it's very faint.'

Ryan nodded. 'So why take another X-ray?'

Toby gave him a wary smile. 'To convince you?'

The consultant laughed. 'I don't need convincing. I know she's got a fracture. I just wanted to be sure you did. Go ahead and get it plastered—you do know how to do that?'

Toby nodded, explained the angle the hand would be held at and the arrangement of the thumb, and Ryan let him go.

Sally helped with the plastering, and she had to admit that Toby did it well. No doubt the orthopaedic team would want to redo it in a few days but, watching him apply the cast, she wasn't sure it would be necessary.

Perhaps Nick's faith in him was justified.

She checked her watch. Almost lunchtime, and then at three, if all went well, she could escape and go shopping and have her butterflies about tonight in peace.

Yet again she wondered what Nick was going to say, and yet again she failed to come to a conclusion. She'd just have to possess her soul in patience, but patience wasn't Sally's strong suit.

The day dragged interminably…

CHAPTER SEVEN

NICK arrived on the stroke of seven-thirty, bearing a bottle of wine and a bunch of flowers from the supermarket near his house. As he walked up the path Sally put the finishing touches to the table, wiped her hands nervously on the sides of her skirt and went to the door, opening it just as the bell rang.

He handed her the wine and the flowers, and she looked at them and tried to see if there was a message in them for her, some symbolic meaning, but there was none.

The flowers weren't red roses—they were a mixed summer bouquet, according to the care label—and the wine, instead of being champagne, was a good robust Italian red.

How had he known it was pasta?

Because it was always pasta? She put the wine down on the side in the kitchen, dumped the flowers in the sink for a moment and stirred the sauce. 'There's a corkscrew there in that drawer,' she told him, indicating it with a jerk of her head.

He sniffed. 'I can smell the garlic from here,' he said with a chuckle, fishing about in the drawer. 'You always did that.'

She put the lid back on with a little bang. She wasn't in the mood for memory lane. She wasn't in the mood for anything, actually, except finding out what this was all in aid of. She turned to him.

118

'Nick, what's this about?' she asked, finally losing her patience.

His smile was wry. 'Let's sit down with a glass of wine over our meal and—'

'No. Let's talk about it now. I may not want to eat.'

'You'll want to eat. I just want to talk about what happened yesterday morning, and I don't want to go in cold.'

She turned off the heat under the sauce, flicked the switch on the kettle to bring it to the boil and grabbed two glasses. 'Open that and come through. I'll be in the sitting room.'

It only took him a moment to join her, but by the time he was there her insides were in knots. She was on the sofa, and he came and sat next to her, pouring the wine and handing her a glass.

Then he settled back in the other corner of the sofa with his glass and took a slow sip before setting it down again.

'Well?' she asked impatiently.

'I think we nearly did something very silly yesterday,' he began. 'I don't know about you but, after seeing Amy's grave, I was raw inside. I needed comfort, oblivion, some kind of emotional release, and you were there. They call it affirmation of life, don't they? That's why there are so many babies born during wars.'

He looked down at his hands. 'Whatever triggered it, I never intended it to happen. I know it might have looked as if I'd planned it, but I really didn't. I was just acknowledging the power of whatever it seems to be between us, and I wasn't wrong, was I?'

She shook her head slowly, and he went on, 'At the time it seemed right, but then afterwards, when I thought about it, I began to doubt our motives.'

'I had no motive,' she told him honestly. 'I just wanted to be with you.'

Nick's eyes darkened and he looked away. 'I wanted you, too, Sally, but it would have been a lousy reason to restart our affair,' he said in a low voice. 'We had it all once, and we made a mess of it. Maybe this is another chance for us, but not as lovers, just as friends. I care a lot about you. I don't want to see you get hurt again.'

And you'll hurt me, she thought with fatalistic acceptance. You don't do commitment. You don't do long term. Sticking power isn't in your vocabulary.

'Well?'

She blinked hard. He kept saying this friends thing. Maybe she really ought to believe him. She dredged up a smile. 'OK. Friends it is. That's better, actually. It means I can criticise you without repercussions.'

He looked surprised for a moment, then gave a little laugh. 'Criticise?' he asked cautiously.

'Yeah. That shirt, for instance, could have done with a press.'

He glanced down and smiled wryly. 'You're lucky I've got a clean one, never mind pressed. And I don't have a clue where the iron is.'

'Scandalous. You've been moved in—what, three, four days now? I would have expected you to redecorate it from top to bottom in that time.'

He smiled and took the wineglass from her hand and put it down, then opened his arms. 'Come here,' he said softly. 'I could really use a hug.'

So could I, she thought sadly, and let him take her in his arms. His chest was hard and solid under her cheek, and she could smell the combination of soap and man that made him uniquely Nick. Maybe friendship did have its advantages, she thought, and nestled closer to him.

No demands, no risks, no guilt trips about not ironing his shirts or putting too much garlic in the spaghetti sauce.

No one to snuggle up to in the wee small hours of the night. No one to tell if things went wrong and you needed a shoulder to cry on—

No, that wasn't true. She could still cry on his shoulder—except he was the thing most likely to go wrong, and he'd just made sure he couldn't, so maybe she wouldn't even need that option.

She lifted her head and cradled his jaw in her hand. 'Supper?' she murmured, and he smiled, just the merest ghost of a smile, and nodded.

'That would be lovely. I was beginning to think you'd got me over here under false pretences.'

'Actually, it's poisoned.'

'So nothing new, then?'

She thumped his chest—just gently—and straightened up. 'I need to cook the pasta. Stay there for a moment, I won't be long. Have another glass of wine.'

'That's my last, if I'm driving,' he told her.

'You don't have to. You can stay. I've got a spare room.'

'I'll go. I seem to have acquired a cat—it's a stray, apparently, and it comes and sits on the stool in the kitchen and miaows at me until I feed it.'

'And, of course, you don't.'

Nick looked guilty.

'It's probably somebody's perfectly well-fed and much loved pet. Is it thin?'

He grinned and shook his head. 'Oh, no. Everyone feeds him, apparently, but my cat flap doesn't lock, so I can't keep him out.'

'Stand something in front of it.'

'It's in the back door.'

'So nail it up!' Sally said, exasperated, and he looked even more guilty and sheepish.

'Actually, he's good company. He sits on the window-sill in the sitting room and watches the birds, and he likes having his ears scratched.'

'Fleas,' Sally said pragmatically, and headed for the kitchen. He was clearly a lost cause, and there was no point reasoning with him. Anyway, it might be better if he didn't stay here overnight. Temptation and all that, and she might do something stupid—like sleepwalk.

She boiled the kettle for the third time, put the water in the pan, threw in the fresh spaghetti from the supermarket and gave it a stir, then checked the sauce.

Was it a bit heavy on garlic? Probably, but God forbid she should admit to it!

Feeling much happier, she drained the pasta, swirled it with olive oil and basil, put it into a plain white serving bowl and carried it through on a tray with the sauce.

'Supper,' she said to him, and he unfolded himself from the sofa and headed towards the table, the wine-glasses and bottle dangling from his fingertips. He set them down in amongst the salad and dressings and Parmesan slivers on the table, and met her eyes.

'OK?' he asked.

She smiled. 'OK,' she confirmed, and pulled out her chair. 'Sit, eat, before it gets cold. And save room for the pudding. It's your favourite.'

'Not your raspberry almond torte?' he said, his eyes lighting up, and she laughed softly.

'Only if you're good. Eat up, and don't complain about the garlic.'

Nick didn't say a word, and by the time he went, she was beginning to think they might be able to do it. It had been a pleasant evening, and they'd talked about old friends and reminisced without getting maudlin.

Well, not too maudlin, anyway.

Sally went to bed alone, and thought of him in his new house with the lost iron and the visiting cat, and fell asleep with a smile on her face before her tears had even dried.

The next few days were fine. Nick was friendly, but kept his distance, and although she missed his little winks and all the sneaking up on her he'd done, it did make working in the department much easier again.

A lot of the tension of the previous week had dissipated, and Sally found she could concentrate on the job, particularly when they were working together on a patient in Resus and teamwork was everything.

She just seemed to know exactly what he wanted and when, and their procedures were seamless.

Even Ryan noticed it, and mentioned it to her at the start of the following week.

'Did you two work together before?' he asked, and she laughed.

'Well—sort of. I was a staff nurse, he was a medical student in his last clinical year.'

Ryan pursed his lips and nodded thoughtfully. 'I would have said you'd worked in a team—you seem to know each other's moves so well.'

Only in bed, she could have said, but she didn't. 'Just a lucky fit,' she said. 'Sometimes you gel, sometimes you don't. I can't work with you or Matt like that, but Matt and Meg seem to gel, and you and Angela have a rapport.'

He shrugged. 'I suppose. It just seems—I don't know. A bit special.'

Tell me about it, Sally thought. Maybe it was something to do with Nick, though, because he seemed to be able to get the best out of Toby as well.

The next day they had an admission, a man in his forties who had woken with a bit of a headache and then been brought in by ambulance complaining of shaking and buzzing in the head and giddiness.

'Get a history,' Nick said to Toby. 'Anything you think might be relevant. Talk to his wife, she will have seen it from the other side. Then come and have a chat about what we do next. Sally, could you go with him and do an ECG while we establish the rest of the facts?'

'Sure.'

She found a portable ECG machine and wheeled it into the cubicle, just as Toby was settling down to take the history. The man seemed quite calm and didn't look too bad, but from his wife's description he had made a huge improvement over the past hour.

He complained of a headache starting over the left side, and a great buzzing and roaring in the head, and violent shaking.

'I thought I was going to fall on the floor,' he explained. 'I had to hang onto the table.'

'He looked awful,' his wife chipped in. 'Grey and waxy. I just knew something bad was wrong. It was much more than just a headache. That's why I dialed 999.'

Toby nodded, making notes, as Sally put monitor leads on the patient's chest. 'Your blood pressure's quite high—is that normal?'

'Yes—I'm on beta-blockers.'

'And what about your pulse rate? That's a bit on the slow side.'

'It always is. I can't get it high, even when I exercise. That's the beta-blockers, I think.'

'Could be.' Toby jotted again, and then did a quick physical survey, flashing a light in the man's eyes one at a time, testing for basic dexterity and strength in the hands and fingers, and then he put the penlight into his pocket and stood up.

'OK. We're just going to run the ECG, and we could do with a urine sample to test, if you could manage to produce one for us in a minute?'

Sally left them with a bottle and the ECG running, and came out of the cubicle in time to hear Toby running through the man's symptoms with Nick.

'So what's your diagnosis?' Nick asked.

Toby looked puzzled. 'I don't know. It could be all sorts of things. It could be migraine, but he doesn't seem to have had any flashing lights, or it could be because his heart beats so slowly—it's under forty beats a minute, and if it dipped, might that have caused it? It could be epilepsy, but there's no history. It could be a CVA of some sort—a clot, a haemorrhage—but it's confusing.'

'How is he now?'

'Tired, a bit shocky.'

Nick nodded, studying the notes again and pursing his lips. 'Any history of migraine?'

'No. Nothing. His mother had it, so he knows what it is.'

'Might be late onset,' Nick mused, but Toby didn't look convinced.

'His wife kept talking about the shaking. I may be crazy, but it sounded almost like Parkinson's. She was emphatic that he wasn't fitting, and there was no loss of consciousness.'

Nick's brow creased in a frown of concentration. 'Any sensory or motor loss? Strength, co-ordination, dexterity?'

'Not that I could detect, but he's very alert. It might be a very minor CVA.'

'Or the start of a major bleed,' Nick said thoughtfully. 'I want to see him. I don't like the sound of it. You'd better come with me.'

It was more than an hour before their patient was transferred to the medical admissions unit, and by that time a physician had been informed of the slight loss of co-ordination and strength on the left-hand side and he'd ordered an MRI scan.

'It may not show anything, of course,' Nick warned as the man was wheeled away.

'I know. It's odd, though—he said the headache was on the left,' Toby muttered, 'and yet the weakness is on the left, too. Strokes cross over, don't they?'

'Usually. Not always,' Nick told him. 'If it's in the cerebellar cortex, it's already crossed, and if it's a co-ordination problem, that could be where it is. We won't know till the scan result comes through. I'll try and find out what happens, but you did a good job on the history—very thorough and thoughtful. Well done.'

Toby seemed to grow in front of their eyes. Grinning, he went off to tackle his next patient, and Sally smiled at Nick. 'That was nice.'

'What?'

'Telling him he'd done well.'

'Don't you do that with your nurses?' he asked, and she smiled again.

'Of course.'

'Well, then. How about coffee?'

She returned his smile. 'Sounds good.'

It was obviously a week for staff morale boosting, Sally thought later the next day when she found Sophie in tears in the loo.

'What's wrong?' she asked, putting an arm round the girl's shoulders and hugging her gently. 'Sophie, talk to me. What's happened?'

'My grandmother,' she sobbed. 'She's got pneumonia, and now they've found she's got a bad heart, and they think she's dying.'

'Oh, Sophie,' Sally murmured, and held her while she cried, then gave her tissues to blot herself up and took her into her office for a chat. 'Do you need time off?' she asked, but Sophie shook her head.

'No, she lives in Audley. She's in a house just round the corner. I see her every evening. I think she ought to go into a home, but the family don't agree. They think I should give up work and look after her, but I can't do that. I expect you think I'm heartless, don't you? Anyway, if I spend a bit of time with her at night, I can look after her *and* work, so it's all right.'

And you probably don't have much other social life, Sally thought. No doubt the family all leant heavily on her, as she was a nurse. It had happened when her grandmother had had a stroke, and all the family had seemed to think that Sally would give up her job and look after her.

She would have done, of course, if it had been practical, but she had to live, and pay her mortgage, and her grandmother hadn't had enough to keep herself afloat, never mind Sally. She'd gone into a home near her two sons in Devon, and her daughter, Sally's mother, had moved down to be near her.

Sally missed them all, but it was the way it had worked out, and apart from any financial consideration, she didn't have the mental reserves to sit with an elderly relative who didn't recognise her, twenty-four hours a day.

It wasn't why she'd trained, and it wasn't where she could do the most good, and she was glad it was the way it was. She explained her own situation to Sophie, and pointed out that the girl had a great deal to offer a great many people, and she should think very carefully before doing anything rash or wearing herself out burning the candle at both ends and in the middle.

'No one person can look after a sick, dependent relative twenty-four hours a day,' she reminded her. 'You can only be effective for some of the time, and then you start to get resentful and unhappy, and it all goes pear-shaped. Anyway, perhaps she'll be admitted and assessed, and your family will understand the need for proper care,' she said reassuringly.

Sophie gave a short laugh. 'I doubt it. My family all think I should be with her, and if anything happens, I know they'll all think it's my fault.'

'Well, just so long as you know you're doing the right thing for all of you. Right, I want you to come with me and do some triage. We've got a build-up in the waiting room, so we need to prioritise. I'd rather have a triage nurse on all the time, but we're too short-staffed to permit it. If I could train you and leave you there, I would, but the danger is until you've seen all the cases a few thousand times, you're likely to miss some vital little snippet that could make all the difference.'

She showed Sophie the triage assessment form, which asked for basic details of the condition the patient was presenting with, and gave a set of boxes for the nurse to tick according to urgency.

'Head injuries, chest pain and things that could be potentially life-threatening come out at the top of the list, ingrowing toenails come bottom. Anyone bleeding copiously is high up because they tend to pass out and, anyway, they make a lot of mess; children tend to be accelerated because things can deteriorate

very fast in little children and nobody likes to see
them suffer. And that's it, really.'

'Is that all?' Sophie said with a strangled laugh. 'I
wouldn't know where to begin!'

'Take a history,' Sally advised. 'Quite brief. Bear
in mind these are the walking wounded. Anyone really bad will have been brought in horizontal. Look
at the patients, assess their condition and how they're
coping. Are they in great pain, or are they managing
to deal with it? Are they going to get much worse if
they have to wait? Some conditions, like burns, need
treating as quickly as possible for the best outcome.'

'I can quite see why you can't leave me here,'
Sophie said, wide-eyed. 'I had no idea it was so involved.'

'You'll get the hang of it,' Sally assured her.
'Right, shall we start?'

They spent an hour doing it, Sally explaining after
each patient left for the waiting room just why they'd
been given the category they had, and by the end
Sophie's judgement had improved hugely.

'You're beginning to get the hang of it,' Sally told
her with a big smile, and Sophie pulled a comic face.

'I'm not sure. It's very difficult.'

'You're doing fine,' Sally assured her. 'Right, let's
let Meg take over, and we'll go and treat some of
them.'

It had been a highly productive day, Sally thought at
the end of it. She'd made some real progress with
Sophie, and she could see that with experience she'd
make an outstanding nurse—always assuming her

family didn't insist she give up her promising career to look after her ailing grandmother.

'You're looking pleased with yourself,' Nick said as she was leaving.

'Good day. How about you?'

'OK. I found out about our headache patient, by the way. The SHO up on the MAU tried to tell me it was migraine, so I rubbed his nose in the notes and sent him back to his boss. He's had an MRI scan now, and he's actually had two strokes, one in the right parietal lobe, the other in the left cerebellar cortex—which explains the pain and buzzing on the left, of course, and also some of the conflicting neurological messages.'

'So what will they do now?' she asked.

'Anticoagulation therapy, and finding out why a comparatively young man in reasonable health should suddenly start getting blood clots. Still, at least he's getting proper treatment now because of Toby's thoroughness.'

'You would have picked it up,' she said confidently, but he shrugged.

'Maybe, maybe not. That's what I mean about him being a good diagnostician. He's not blinkered. He'll look at something and say if it doesn't fit, and then look again.'

'And how's his lady with heart failure?'

'She had a massive pulmonary embolus,' he told her. 'They found it at post-mortem.'

'Ah.'

'Yes, ah. It wouldn't have made any difference if she'd had the injection. In fact, it might have saved her a great deal of pain. Never mind, these things happen. You going home?'

She nodded. 'Yes—only half an hour late. What about you?'

'I am, too. I've got study leave this afternoon, supposedly. I'll walk you to your car.'

'How gentlemanly.'

'Not really, I'm going that way anyway,' he said with a grin.

She laughed. Nick was always such fun to have around, so silly and light-hearted and cheering. 'How's the house?' she asked.

'Oh, fine. I seem to have a permanent resident, though.'

'The cat?'

He nodded. 'Winston. He's black and he sits on the window-sill and eyeballs the neighbourhood. He's a good friend—well, mostly. Yesterday morning he puked on the carpet.'

'Oh, gorgeous,' she said with a chuckle. 'Never mind, you didn't like the carpet all that much anyway.'

'I didn't mind. I just thought it was a bit patchy. That might, of course, be why!' He looked at his watch, then back at Sally.

'I don't suppose you fancy joining me for a barbecue tonight, do you? I'm getting fed up with eating on my own, and it's such a lovely afternoon.'

'What about your study leave?' she asked, reluctant to interfere with the progress of his career.

'Oh, I can do something later. Flexi-hours, you know?'

'I know,' she replied, thinking of how her housework and gardening tended to get flexed into sporadic bursts. She ought to be doing some washing tonight, but the idea of a barbecue with Nick was so tempting...

'You don't have to stay late,' he coaxed, and she felt herself weakening.

'Just so long as you do some of your study,' she bargained.

He agreed. 'You can wash up, if you like,' he suggested. 'That will make it even fairer.'

As Sally drove over there later, she thought that this friendship thing seemed to be working very well. She'd missed having him in her life, and this gave her his companionship without the threat of emotional trauma, because her heart wasn't going to be broken when their affair ended.

Quite how she'd feel if there was another woman in his life was a bridge she'd cross if and when they ever reached it. She just hoped, for her sake, that it didn't happen. Certainly there seemed no sign of it at present.

She arrived at five, just in time to help turn the kebabs and sausages on the barbecue and throw together a salad, and after a couple of hours of light-hearted banter and camaraderie, she left him and went home and tackled her washing.

Yes, this friendship thing could work very well, she thought as she lay down and snuggled under the quilt, but when she woke in the night, it was to the lingering whisper of a dream, and her arms were so empty they ached...

CHAPTER EIGHT

NICK was finding the friendship thing a nightmare. If he hadn't had such iron self-discipline he wouldn't have coped. As it was, he limped along, eaten alive by frustration and wondering if he was completely mad to have suggested it.

In his heart, though, he knew he was right. He'd hurt Sally. He'd only just recently found out quite how much, and it tortured him. There was no way he could risk hurting her again, and if that meant staying away from her, then he'd have to do that.

Even if it meant altering the whole course of his career.

He found Ryan in the staffroom, mourning over the dregs of the coffee, and he put another pot on to brew. While they were waiting, Ryan asked him how he was getting on.

'Oh, fine. It's a good place to work.'

'You and Sally seem to mesh.'

His eyes seemed to see too much, and Nick turned his attention back to the coffee-machine. 'We do, don't we?' he said noncommittally. He decided to change the subject, fast. 'Is there a good florist round here? I need to buy some flowers for someone.'

He missed the flicker of interest in Ryan's eyes, and there was no hint of it in the man's reply.

'Just round the corner in the main entrance—they're excellent. They deliver, or you can pick up.

It's a little independent local firm, and they've got a couple of branches in the town, too.'

Nick nodded. 'Thanks. I'll pay them a visit. Coffee?'

Ryan shrugged away from the wall and held out his mug. 'Thanks. So, have you given any more thought to my suggestion?'

Nick poured the coffee and stalled his answer for a moment, then said, 'The jury's still out. Is that OK? How long have I got?'

'A few more weeks? We'll be advertising in October.'

It was the third week in August. Nick added milk to his coffee and retreated to the chairs. 'OK. I'll let you know in a week or two,' he said, and adroitly changed the subject.

'How's your grandmother?'

Sophie looked up from the trolley she was laying and smiled wearily at Sally. 'Oh, OK. The community nurse is going in three times a day, and I'm staying there at night now.'

'Don't get overtired,' Sally warned. 'That's your boss speaking now. You need to be alert to do your job, and I can't let you continue if I think you're too tired to do it properly, so be careful.'

It was a gentle warning, but meant. Sally knew only too well how easy it was to get overtired. She was finding sleep elusive, and it did make it harder to concentrate and keep a clear head.

Later that day they had an emergency admission, an elderly lady who had collapsed in the street. She was suffering from mild chest pain, but her breathing was poor and Sally put her on oxygen before fetching Nick to see her.

Sophie was with her, and together they made her more comfortable, loosening her clothing and removing her blouse and a ridiculously tight and heavily upholstered long-line bra which was almost cutting off her circulation.

'Oh, that's better,' she gasped, panting as she relaxed against the backrest. 'Oh, what a relief!'

'I should think so, it's a ghastly instrument of torture,' Sally told her with a smile, slipping her arms into a little modesty top and covering her with a blanket. 'I'll just set up the ECG machine so we can get a look at your ticker—ah, here's Dr Baker.'

Nick took the lady's hand and smiled down at her, and Sally thought it was a wonder she didn't just die of heart failure on the spot. Instead, she smiled back.

'Right, tell me all about it. When did this start?'

'I was shopping,' she said, and paused for breath. 'I had a pain. I sat down for a bit. It didn't get better, so I spoke to the staff—they said they'd call an ambulance. It was better by the time they came, though.'

'Where is the pain?' he asked, and she pointed to the centre of her chest, and then moved her hand over her left shoulder and down her arm.

'Sort of all over, really. I can feel it—oh, it's coming back again. Oh, no.'

She pressed a hand to the centre of her chest and her face creased in pain. 'Oh, Doctor, it's worse. Oh, it hurts!'

'Can we get these leads on?' Nick snapped, and within seconds she was linked up to the monitor and he was frowning at the screen. The trace was changing as they watched, Q-waves forming, indicating an MI.

'OK, my darling, I think you're having a bit of a heart attack,' Nick explained gently. 'Don't worry, we'll give you something to make you more comfortable. Sally, let's have 5 mg diamorphine with 12.5 mg Stemetil IV, stat.'

Sophie handed him a cannula and he had the line in and taped down by the time Sally had the drugs drawn up. The woman's relief was gradual but definite, and Sally noticed that Sophie was doing a wonderful job of soothing her. She was stroking her head, helping her by holding the oxygen mask just off her face because the pressure was upsetting her, and by the time the diamorphine had been slowly delivered, she was a little calmer.

She looked awful, though, clammy and grey, and there was a bluish tinge around her lips. Nick obviously agreed. 'Right, she needs to go straight up to CCU.'

But their patient wasn't waiting for the coronary care unit. Without any further warning, her heart stopped.

'Damn,' Nick muttered, and flicked the backrest out from behind her, dropping her flat, while Sally kicked the brakes off the trolley.

'Resus One,' Nick snapped, and they rushed her into the emergency treatment room and commenced CPR, while Sophie stood helplessly in the background.

'Let's shock her. Stand back.'

The woman arched and flopped, and Nick shook

his head as he studied the monitor. 'Nothing. Let's turn it up.'

Still there was no response.

'I need atrophine and adrenaline,' Nick said, and fired off a list of instructions at Sophie, who was looking stunned.

Sally rescued her. 'I'll do it. Sophie, take over here. Squeeze the bag once every five compressions.'

She drew up the drugs and handed the tray with the syringe in to Nick, but Sophie turned and bumped into the tray, nearly knocking it out of Sally's hand.

'Oh—sorry!' she said, and Nick shot her a black look.

'It's all right, Sophie, no harm done,' Sally murmured reassuringly, and sent Nick a black look of her own that he didn't see.

Sophie, shaken and upset, had returned to her ambu-bag and was religiously counting to five and then squeezing.

The next ten minutes were hectic and futile, and finally Nick gave a heavy sigh. He straightened up and looked at Sally. 'Why are we doing this?' he said softly.

She gave him an understanding smile. 'Because you can't give up until you've given it everything you've got?'

He dropped his head forwards and shut his eyes, then peeled the tape off the giving set and took the cannula out of her arm. 'Poor old girl. We didn't even know her name.'

'Ethel,' Sophie said quietly. 'She was Ethel.'

And she burst into tears.

'Give me a minute,' Sally murmured, and she

steered Sophie out of Resus and down to the privacy of her office.

'Bit close to home, was it?' she said sympathetically, and Sophie hiccuped and nodded.

'She was just like my grandma,' she said, sobbing again. 'It was awful.'

'I know.' Sally hugged her and rubbed Sophie's shoulders soothingly until she'd got herself back under control, then she took her into the staffroom and plied her with coffee. 'You'll be all right. Take a few minutes off, OK?'

She nodded, and Sally left her and went back to Resus, where Nick was tidying up Ethel.

'How is she?' he asked, and Sally shrugged.

'Upset. Ethel reminded her of her grandmother.'

He paused and pulled a face. 'Oh, dear. When did she die?'

'She didn't, but she's probably just about to,' Sally told him. 'You were a bit hard on her, Nick.'

'I didn't say a word!'

'You didn't need to. That look was enough, but I don't think she saw it.'

'Whatever, she's clumsy and incompetent.'

'No, she's learning. There's a difference. Anyway, she was upset.'

'Life's a bitch, you have to get used to it,' he murmured, just as Meg popped her head round the door.

'There's a lady here looking for her mother—Ethel Bailey? Said she collapsed in the street. Is she your patient?' She glanced at the body lying on the trolley, and her mouth formed an O. 'I'll put her in the relatives' room, shall I, with a cup of tea?'

'I'll come,' Nick said, and looked at Sally.

'Can you finish getting her ready?'

She nodded, and while he went and told Ethel's daughter the news, Sally combed her hair and eased the lines of stress from Ethel's face, so that when the daughter saw her she looked at peace.

Sophie should have been here, she thought, instead of being left with the memory of the resuscitation attempts. As soon as she was able to get away, she went down to the staffroom, but she'd gone.

'She's in cubicle three with a patient,' Meg told her.

'Is she all right?'

'Seems fine. She's doing a dressing for Nick.'

'I'll go and see her,' Sally said, and slipped through the curtain. It was the wrong thing to do, because Sophie turned towards her and her apron caught the edge of the paper towel that the equipment was laid out on and sent some of the things flying.

With a startled exclamation she bent down and picked up the fallen swabs and little trays, and to Sally's dismay she put them back on the trolley in amongst the sterile equipment.

'No!' Sally warned, but Nick was quicker.

He muttered an oath under his breath and pointed at the curtain. 'Out,' he said firmly. 'If you don't understand the basic principles of asepsis, you don't work with me. I can't have that kind of clumsiness and stupidity near my patients. Sister Clarke, take over, please.'

Sophie, aghast, sent Sally an agonised look before running from the cubicle in tears, and without a word Sally stepped up beside Nick, cleared away the contaminated dressing pack and opened another, conscious of his scrutiny.

Let him watch, she thought furiously. There was nothing wrong with her aseptic technique, it was probably better than his. She snapped the gloves on, turned to the patient and dredged up a smile. 'Hi, there,' she said cheerfully. 'This shouldn't hurt, but it might be cold.'

She cleaned the wound, a nasty scrape up the front of his shin, stood back so Nick could examine it, and then, after he was satisfied that it was clean, she dressed it while he watched her every move.

'There. Better?' she asked the patient, and he nodded.

Nick gave him instructions for follow-up and a prescription for antibiotics, and sent him on his way.

'Right, what's next?' he said.

Sally shut the door behind their patient and turned to Nick, finally letting her temper show. 'How *dare* you criticise one of my nurses in front of a patient?' she said, her voice deadly quiet.

He looked stunned for a second, but he bounced back fast enough. 'Oh, come on, Sal, she was out of order! All that stuff was contaminated—'

'Very likely, and I was dealing with it!' she snapped. 'Anyway, you were unnecessarily harsh to her. You know quite well she's still upset about Ethel and her grandmother, you could have been more gentle.'

'That's beside the point. She was about to make a serious mistake,' he cut in, but she glared at him and went on.

'It's *all* beside the point. What we're talking about

here is you exceeding your authority. Quite apart
from the fact that I was there and able to sort it out
myself, you never—ever—do that in front of a patient! If you have a problem with one of my nurses,
you tell me—not her. And if I'm not around and you
feel it's a serious matter, you quietly and discreetly
send the nurse out to find another one to take over,
and then you inform me. You do not tell her off in
front of the patients! Is that understood?'

'Oh, Sally, I hardly told her off—'

'You sent her out, quite clearly in disgrace! You
can't do that!'

Nick sighed harshly and rammed a hand through
his hair. 'You really are being ridiculous—!'

'Don't call me ridiculous! Don't you *dare* call me
ridiculous! What she did wasn't a patch on the howler
your precious Toby was about to make. How would
you have felt if I'd been the one to find him and I'd
spoken to him like that?'

'It was totally different!'

'Yes—and about ten orders of magnitude more sig-
nificant! At the worst this might have resulted in a
minor infection. Toby's error would have been fatal,
and you know it.'

'Oh, come on, Sally,' he reasoned. 'A mistake's a
mistake, we all make them.'

'So Toby just gets a quiet word in his ear because
you're all chaps together, but you can flay Sophie to
shreds because she's only a little nurse? Well, tough,
Nick. She's *my* little nurse, she's a good nurse, and
she's my responsibility. If she needs reprimanding—
which *I* will decide—then *I'll* do it, not you. I want

an apology, and I want it now. Go and find her and say sorry—graciously!'

'Like hell,' he gritted under his breath. 'She was a hazard to that patient's health—'

'And you were out of line. Either you find her and apologise or I go to Ryan about this. Is that clear? And if Toby makes a single tiny error, I'll take that to Ryan, too, only, unlike you, I won't do it in front of the patients!'

She yanked back the curtain and stalked out, and the staff in the corridor melted out of her way.

'Uh-oh,' someone murmured as she strode past, but apart from that there was silence. Fine. She didn't want to talk to anyone anyway—and most particularly not Nick!

She found Sophie sobbing in the staffroom, mopped her up and took her through to her office, sitting her down for a chat.

'Right. Talk to me, Sophie.'

'I just wasn't concentrating,' she wept. 'I was still thinking about Ethel, and my grandma. I didn't think—I just picked them up. I'm sorry. It won't happen again.'

'I'm sure it won't,' she soothed. 'I'm not worried about it, anyway. I know your aseptic technique is fine. What I'm much more worried about is you, and how you're coping with your grandmother. You're looking tired, and it can't go on. It isn't fair on the rest of us if you're running at fifty per cent. We need a full complement up and running to keep this department on its toes, and if you aren't concentrating, you aren't an asset, are you?'

Sophie shook her head miserably.

'Is there anyone else who could be there with your grandmother at night?' Sally suggested.

'Mum? She says I'm better, though, because I'm a nurse, but I'm so tired. She keeps calling me all night.'

'Which means you aren't sleeping,' Sally finished for her. 'Sophie, you've got to talk to your mother. I'm sure they don't want you getting into trouble and making mistakes because you're exhausted, do they?'

She shook her head, and Sally stood up. 'Right. I'm going back to work. I want you with me for the rest of the day, and then you can sort this out when you get home. I want the situation resolved by the end of the week, or you're going to have to take some time off for unpaid leave until it's sorted. OK?'

Sophie nodded, then looked worriedly at the door. 'What about Dr Baker?'

Sally felt her jaw clench, and consciously relaxed it. 'What about Dr Baker? I've dealt with him,' she said crisply, and opened the door to find Nick there, his hand poised to knock.

She gave him an icy look. 'Perfect timing. I'll leave you two together.'

He looked startled and uncomfortable, and Sally was conscious of Sophie panicking behind her, but it was tough. They were both adults, let them deal with it. She walked out, shut the door firmly and left them to it.

'I gather you and Nick had a humdinger earlier,' Ryan said quietly in a moment of sanity later in the day.

'Is that right?' she replied, totally noncommittal.

'So a little bird tells me.'

'The birds round here talk far too much,' she muttered.

Ryan chuckled slightly and cocked his head on one side, studying her thoughtfully. 'Are you OK?'

'I'm fine. I expect he'll live, as well.'

'Ouch.'

She met Ryan's laughing eyes and smiled reluctantly. 'It's OK, Ryan, it's under control. He criticised a nurse.'

'Fatal mistake.'

'Absolutely. He won't do it again. How're Ginny and the kids?'

'Fine.' He smiled knowingly and let her get away with the switch of subject, to her relief. She knew Nick had apologised to Sophie, and as far as she was concerned the subject was now closed.

All she had to do was convince everyone else to stop talking about it—and make her own peace with Nick. That might be more of a challenge, after all the things she'd said.

Sally didn't see him again before she went off duty, and it troubled her. They'd never had a row before that they hadn't resolved, and this one had been left hanging in the air.

She had no idea what kind of atmosphere she'd have to face next time they worked together, although he'd never in the past borne a grudge or kept a row going for the sake of it. She would have thought he'd seek her out and talk to her about it, but he hadn't, and that hurt.

Had he changed? Maybe. It was seven years, and he was much older now in so many ways. Maybe he felt she had no right to correct him in his exalted position as an almost-consultant.

Tough. In her opinion, he should have got his relationships with other members of staff sorted by now.

She cleaned the house, scrubbing away her anger and apprehension, and then fell into bed exhausted at just gone nine. She had an early start the next day—as usual—and if she was going to have to deal with Nick in a grump, she wanted to have all her ducks in a row.

Sally's house was in darkness, and by now everyone else had lights on. Had she gone out? Her car was still there, and he didn't think it very likely that she would have walked anywhere, unless she'd popped into a neighbour's.

'I think she's in,' the lady over the road called. 'She might have gone to bed.'

Nick thanked her, and looked up at the house again. Should he wake her? They'd never parted on a row before—well, only once, and look what had happened then. No. He couldn't leave it overnight.

His mind made up, he rang the doorbell and waited, and after a moment the landing light came on, then the hall light, and he saw Sally running down the stairs.

Without stopping to identify him, she opened the door and stood there in silence. Her face was expressionless.

'Hello, Sally,' he said quietly. 'I'm sorry to wake you. Can I come in?'

For a long moment she hesitated, then she moved

back and held the door. He stepped past her and heard the latch click behind him.

'Come on through,' she said economically.

She led him into the sitting room, but she didn't sit. Instead she stood there, her arms folded defensively, and waited.

'I've come to apologise,' he said, and she arched a brow.

'It wasn't me you needed to apologise to, it was Sophie, and I gather you've done that,' she said, her voice tight, giving nothing away.

Nick sighed and shook his head. 'No. I need to apologise to you as well. You were right. I was out of order. I'm sorry. And I'm sorry I yelled at you.'

For a long while he thought she was going to carry on standing there with that odd look on her face, but then she sighed and looked away and looked back at him, and he could see the shimmer of tears in her eyes. Her voice when she spoke was rough with emotion. 'OK. Thanks.'

So what now? he asked himself. In the old days, after a row, he'd take her in his arms and hug her, and then they'd make love.

They couldn't do that any more, it didn't fit with the friendship thing. Suddenly plagued by uncertainty, he turned towards the door, and her voice stopped him.

'Where are you going?'

He turned back so he could see her face, but she was giving nothing away. 'Home,' he told her. 'It's late. I've already woken you, I don't want to keep you up.'

'Stay for coffee,' she said, and there was a touch of something in her voice that could have been a plea.

He nodded. 'OK.'

'I've got chocolate biscuits.'

He felt his mouth tug in a smile, and hers echoed it, just a tiny, rather uncertain smile that made him ache for all they'd lost. It would be so easy to cross the room and take her in his arms and persuade her to make love, but it would only hurt her. She didn't want it, and he had no right to impose his feelings on her.

Not now.

Not after Amy.

'Chocolate biscuits sound good,' he said, and smiled, and the tension eased from her face a little.

She was really worried about it, he thought, and realised that he had been, too. He perched on one of the high stools at the breakfast bar in her kitchen and watched as she made instant coffee, then drank it without a murmur, dunking chocolate biscuits in it until it was cool enough to drink. And they talked about Sophie's grandmother and how Sophie was working all day and then staying up all night caring for her elderly relative, and he felt even more of a heel and vowed to speak to her the next day.

Then the coffee was finished, and there was no reason to sit there any longer. Putting his mug down, he stood up and patted his pocket for his keys, and Sally slid off her stool and followed him into the hall.

'Would it be exceeding my authority to give you a goodnight hug, Sister Clarke?' he murmured with a rueful smile, and she smiled back and put her arms out and hugged him hard.

'I'm sorry,' she murmured, and he squeezed her gently.

'Don't be. I had it coming.'

'Let's just forget it, can we?'

'Sure.' Nick eased away from her slightly, so that his face was just above hers as she looked up at him, and for a moment he hesitated.

Just one small kiss, his alter ego prodded. What harm can it do?

He did kiss her, but on the cheek, a light brush of his lips against the milk-soft skin, and then he moved away, opening the door and letting himself out.

'Night, Sally. Sleep well,' he said quietly, and then with a dull ache inside that no one else could ease, he drove away from her, back to his empty, lonely house that was crying out for the warmth of her personality.

It wasn't only the house crying out for her, he thought heavily, but there was nothing he could do about it. She didn't want him, and that was that.

He went up to the study, opened his books and stared at them blindly for an hour, then admitted defeat, had a shower and went to bed.

CHAPTER NINE

'So did you get your flowers?'

'Flowers?' Sally looked curiously at Ryan. 'What flowers?'

'Oh—nothing. Nick was asking about a florist— I must have misunderstood.' He looked a little embarrassed, but he wouldn't enlarge on it. In fact, he looked distinctly as if he thought he'd put his foot in it, and it puzzled her for a few minutes.

She hadn't had any flowers—and she didn't have a birthday coming up, neither was it an impending anniversary of anything between them. How odd, she thought, and then the penny finally dropped.

They weren't for her.

He'd wanted to be friends. He'd bought condoms, when there was no likelihood of their relationship taking that particular twist in the road, and he'd been only too happy to backtrack and let her talk them both out of it.

And since then he'd been remarkably circumspect.

He was having an affair. He was having an affair, and he hadn't told her because they were only friends and as such it was none of her darned business.

'Idiot,' she muttered, stalking off down the corridor and hoping she didn't run into him before she'd got her emotions under control. 'That's why he'd bought a house, to be near her. He didn't know you were

150

here, it was just coincidence. Oh, you stupid, stupid fool.'

She hid in her office for a while, as it was reasonably quiet, but after a few minutes there was a tap on the door and Sophie came in. Sally conjured up a smile from somewhere.

'Hi. What can I do for you?'

'Meg needs you—and I wanted to tell you I've sorted it out with Mum.'

Sally blinked at the young nurse. Sorted it out? 'Oh—right. Your grandmother. Tell me,' she said, dragging her mind off Nick and back onto her job.

'Mum's going to stay with her until we can find a home. We spoke to Gran, and she doesn't want to stay in her house any more. She's lonely in the day and frightened at night, and we thought we were doing what she wanted! Silly, isn't it? Anyway, I'm sorry about yesterday, and thanks for being so understanding.'

'Anytime. As they say, been there, done that. So, how busy is it out there at the moment? I just want to get this paperwork up to date—any chance? Does Meg need me now?'

Sophie laughed. 'She does really. It's getting a bit clogged up in the waiting room, and Meg said could you come? There are lots of non-urgent things you could be dealing with, she said.'

'Sure.' She put her pen back in her pocket and followed Sophie out of the office. Just so long as she didn't have to work alongside Nick, she'd be fine.

She found Meg in triage, with a queue, and popped her head round the door.

'It's like buses,' Meg said, rolling her eyes. 'Nothing for ages, then they all come at once. I think they're a bit overwhelmed out the back—any chance I can drag you away from that report to do some suturing and the like?'

Sally chuckled. 'You know I hate writing reports. I'll have to do it some time, but just for now I'm sure I can be persuaded to help.'

She left Meg dealing with her queue of patients, meaning to tackle the less urgent cases in order while Nick and Ryan and the other nurses dealt with the more urgent ones—only, of course, because life was like that, she ended up working alongside Nick instead.

'You OK?' he asked softly in a tiny lull.

'Sure. I'm fine,' she said, and she flashed him a smile and hoped the lie didn't show on her face. It was her own fault. She shouldn't have allowed herself to fall for him again—except she meant still, really, not again, because she'd never got over him the first time.

She should have gone with him to Manchester all those years ago. She knew that now. Then he would have seen Amy, and they would still be together, or at least they would have had the chance, whereas now…

Now he was doing what he'd done all along, found himself an available woman who didn't demand commitment, one who knew the rules. No, she'd done the right thing letting him go to Manchester alone. What she was doing wrong now was letting him get under her skin again.

'Friends,' she muttered, and his brows twitched together.

'Pardon?'

'Nothing. Just thinking aloud. Right, what's next?'

Sally got through the day by being brisk and busi-nesslike, and those that knew her well took a slight step back and kept out of her way. Ryan looked guilty every time she saw him because he'd let the cat out of the bag about the flowers, but it wasn't really his fault. He'd just guessed the wrong woman, obviously.

Oh, well, forewarned was forearmed and all that, so she ought to be grateful to Ryan, really. No doubt Nick would tell her at some point or let it slip, and then she'd just have to feign delight for him.

Damn it, she *should* be delighted for him. She didn't want him to be lonely and unhappy. It was just the thought of him being with someone other than her that hurt so much.

The rest of the week was a little better, because she'd spent a few hours howling to herself and had her emotions more under control. Anyway, they were too busy in the department for her to have time to think, and just when they were running at full stretch, they had a message from the maternity unit to say they were closing down and taking no new admis-sions, because of an outbreak of the MRSA virus.

All maternity admissions now had to be sent to other hospitals, and the maternity block was going to be emptied and sterilised, from the reception area right through to the theatres. Only the outpatients clinics would keep running.

This meant that anyone who was unable to get to another hospital would be funnelled via A and E, and they had an obstetric squad on standby for them.

Not obstetrics, Sally thought wretchedly. Anything but obstetrics. However, they weren't deluged with babies, to her relief. Just the normal run-of-the-mill falls and sprains and cuts and so on, which kept her busy, and then just before lunch one of their regulars stumbled in, clutching a blood-soaked rag to his head and reeking of meths and the great unwashed, and Sally went and retrieved him from Reception where he was making a nuisance of himself and sat him down in a cubicle.

Then, because he was very likely to be a source of all manner of infections, she snapped on a pair of latex gloves.

'Now, Frank,' she said firmly in her best headmistress voice, 'I want you to sit still and let me look at your head.'

'Cut m'self,' he mumbled, and she prised the sodden rag out of his hand and looked at the welling wound on his temple.

'Yes, I can see you have. What on, any idea?'

'Something hit me,' he slurred.

'The pavement, I expect,' Sally muttered under her breath. 'OK, Frank, I'm going to clean it up. This might sting a bit.'

She dabbed cautiously, and he yelled and lashed out at her with a surprisingly strong hand, unbalancing her. She would have fallen but for a pair of equally strong arms that closed around her and held her solidly against a very masculine chest.

'OK?' Nick murmured in her ear, and when she nodded he let her go.

'Right, Frank, let's not fight this, eh?' he said

cheerfully, and crouched down, squinting at the nasty, grubby cut. 'When did you do this?'

''S morning,' he mumbled. 'Fell down.'

'OK, mate, let's get you on the couch, shall we?' Nick said firmly, and helped him out of his coat. 'All right, down you go—that's it.'

'What's that?' Sally asked, pointing at his leg.

'Good grief. Looks like blood—where's that coming from?'

'Leg hurts,' he groaned, and Nick eased the broken top of a bottle out of his trouser pocket and raised an eyebrow.

'OK, Frank, we're just going to take your trousers off. Sal, I think you'd better cut them so we can ease them away from there.'

'He'll love that. I expect these are his best trousers. Still, we've got plenty more in our cupboard and they're cut to shreds anyway.' She started at the hem and snipped carefully all the way up to the waist, and as the material fell away with the tinkle of broken glass, they could see a nasty, oozing gash on his leg.

'There's glass in that, I'm sure,' Nick said in a low undertone. 'We'd better have an X-ray.'

Frank suddenly reared up and looked down at his legs, and lunged at Sally. 'What you doing to me, you mad woman? You cut my trousers up!'

'It's all right, Frank, we'll get you new ones,' she promised, keeping safely out of reach this time. 'Just lie down and keep still or I might cut something else off by accident.'

His eyes widened, and he lay down obediently and remained motionless while she cut up the other trouser leg and peeled the filthy, smelly garment away.

'These, too, I think,' Nick murmured, indicating the stained and reeking underpants, and she snipped them off and dropped them into a bag with the trousers, leaving Frank squirming and indignant on the couch.

'Here—preserve your modesty,' she said, tucking a blanket round him but leaving his leg exposed.

'I think I might admit him,' Nick said thoughtfully. 'Twenty-four hours in here to dry out and have a good scrub would do you the world of good, don't you think, Frank?'

'Not staying here—they'll cut my clothes off while I'm asleep!' he said, clutching at the blanket.

'He won't stay,' Sally told him. 'He never does. Just get the glass out if you can, sew him up and send him home.'

'Has he got one?'

'Oh, yes. You've got a nice little house, haven't you, Frank? You just don't spend much time in it. You'd rather be here with us.'

He snorted, and Nick filled out the X-ray request and went off to deal with another patient, chuckling under his breath.

The X-ray showed a couple of shards of glass deep in the cut, and while Sally cleaned up Frank's head and stuck the edges of the cut together with Steristrips, Nick gave him a local anaesthetic and dug about in the cut on his leg until he'd found the glass, compared the little slivers to the film and declared himself satisfied.

'I'll let you sew him up,' he said cheerfully to Sally, and she rolled her eyes and settled down to stitch it. Frank, for once, made it easy for her by passing out and snoring loudly, and she then had the difficult task of waking him to send him home.

She and Sophie gave him a blanket bath while they had him there, ostensibly to cut down infection round the wound in his leg, and then they found him new pants and socks and trousers from their clothing cupboard.

'Don't suppose there's a shirt, is there?' Frank asked hopefully, and Sally had to admit the one he was wearing had seen better days. They found him a fresh one with more life in it, and then she gave him a penicillin injection and a tetanus booster and sent him off to the pharmacy to get his prescription.

'Do you think he'll get it?' Sophie asked, and Sally shrugged.

'I doubt it. He's probably found a cleaning cupboard open and nicked the meths out of it already.'

Sophie chuckled, but Sally meant every word. Frank was a worry, and one day he'd come to a sticky and untimely end. Still, there was nothing they could do but put him back together again until, like Humpty Dumpty, all the king's horses and all the king's men didn't have the technology.

'This place reeks,' Sally said, wrinkling her nose, and she called the domestic staff to come and douse the place with disinfectant and clean it from end to end.

'Right, I've had enough of this,' she announced. 'I'm going to take over from Meg and do some triage while she has lunch.'

'Don't you want lunch?' Sophie asked, and she laughed.

'After Frank? I'd gag if I tried to eat. Maybe later when the smell's worn off.'

She chivvied Meg out of the triage room and took over, and dealt with a steady trickle of non-urgent and minor injuries. She was beginning to think she'd been better off at the back when there was a diversion that completely took her breath away.

Nick was busy in Resus, working with Angela after a little sleight of hand on Sally's behalf, and she was just restocking the gauze pads and paper towels when a familiar middle-aged woman walked in and hesitated.

She was obviously looking for something or someone, and Sally was just racking her brains to work out who she was when the woman turned and caught sight of her.

'Sally!' she exclaimed, and then a smile that she would have recognised anywhere lit up those too-familiar blue eyes, and the penny dropped.

'Mrs Baker! Hi—how are you?'

Nick's mother wrapped her in a hug and kissed her cheek, then held her at arm's length and studied her. 'Oh, you haven't changed a bit! Oh, Sally, it's so nice to see you, I was hoping you'd be here. I've just popped in on my way back from Norwich airport to say hello to Nick, and I can't stay more than a few minutes, but I'm glad I've had a chance to see you.'

'Me, too,' Sally said warmly, and drew her into the triage room, shutting the door. 'Have a seat for a minute. Nick's in Resus, he may well be a few minutes. I'd take you in the staffroom but I can't abandon my post. Can I get you a cup of tea?'

She shook her head. 'No, I'm fine. I'd rather spend

the time talking to you.' She leant forwards and squeezed Sally's arm. 'Of all his girlfriends over the years, you've always been my favourite.'

Sally laughed a little awkwardly. 'I can't imagine why, after I broke up with him.'

'What, because you refused to trail after him like a puppy? You had your own career. If it hadn't been for his stubborn pride I think you would have been together now. You should have been, I think. You were right for each other. He hasn't been happy since, you know.'

Sally wondered if Mrs Baker knew about the mistress, but she kept quiet. It was none of her business and, anyway, she didn't have proof.

Nick's mother fiddled with her keyring for a moment, then she looked up again and her eyes were over-bright. 'He told me about the baby, Sally,' she said gently. 'I'm so sorry—you shouldn't have had to go through that alone.'

The grief that was never completely forgotten brought a sad smile to Sally's lips. 'I wasn't alone,' she corrected, touched by Mrs Baker's concern. 'I had my mother. She was wonderful.'

'You should have had Nick.'

'I know. Still, we can't turn back the clock.' She glanced through the glass panel in the door and saw a patient enter the department. 'Look, I'm sorry, I have to deal with someone. Can I point you at the staffroom and tell Nick you're here? He'll come and see you as soon as he can.'

'Sure, of course. And it is lovely to see you again. I hope I'll be seeing more of you.'

Sally dredged up a smile. 'Probably,' she lied,

knowing it was unlikely. When Mrs Baker had left for the staffroom, Sally stuck her head round the door in Resus and told Nick his mother was there, and went back to her post.

Half an hour later she saw her leave, and then Nick appeared.

'Thanks for looking after her. Bit quiet round here, isn't it?'

'Don't tempt fate,' she warned. 'It's about time, it's been chaos for days and we don't need another Frank. My stomach's still churning.'

He smiled, his eyes creasing slightly, and the ache in her heart intensified. He perched a hip on her desk and looked down at her searchingly. 'You look tired,' he said bluntly.

She pulled a face. 'Gee, thanks. I feel so much better now.'

'Sorry, but you do. Is everything all right?'

No, but there's nothing you can do, she thought. Our baby's dead, you're having an affair—life's just a peach, really. 'Everything's fine,' she assured him. 'I'm going to take a break before it gets busy again.'

She stood up, her leg brushing his, and heat shot up it at the unexpected contact. 'I'll join you,' he said, defeating the object, but there was nothing she could say. Still, it was after two o'clock. She could escape soon.

She got through her hasty teabreak by making small talk about his mother, and then, leaving the last few mouthfuls of tea, she went back to the triage room, just as a car pulled up outside and a hugely pregnant woman struggled out of it, a towel clutched between her legs.

'Oh, no,' Sally muttered under her breath. 'Here we go.'

She grabbed a wheelchair and went to meet them in the ambulance bay.

'I'm—having my baby,' the woman gasped. 'I rang—they said the unit was shut, but I can't wait.'

'It's OK,' Sally assured her, and turned to the husband. 'If you could quickly put your car in the car park, I'll take your wife in and make her more comfortable, all right?'

'Fine. Her name's Linda, by the way. Linda Field.'

'Thanks. OK, Linda, let's go and sort you out.' She flashed him a smile, dragged the wheelchair down to one of the more private cubicles away from the waiting area and beckoned to Nick on the way past.

He arched a brow, disappeared into the stores for an obstetrics pack and reappeared just as she'd helped the woman up onto the bed. She propped the backrest up, stripped off Linda's trousers and underwear and covered her with a blanket.

'This is Linda,' she told Nick. 'Her waters broke a few minutes ago, she's contracting every three minutes.'

'Hello, Linda.' He perched on the edge of the bed and smiled reassuringly at her. 'Don't worry, you're in safe hands. How many babies have you had, or is this your first?'

'Three—and they always come fast. I would have had it at home, but my midwife's out on another delivery because of the unit shutting, and I thought it was better to come here.'

'Better to be on the safe side,' Nick agreed, quickly

washing his hands and pulling on gloves. 'Sally, have you got obstetrics qualifications?'

She shook her head. 'No. Have you?'

He smiled. 'Oh, yes. I don't think we're going to have a problem, so long as you don't mind me playing midwife.'

Linda shook her head and laughed a little desperately. 'I don't care who delivers it, just so long as someone does and it isn't before my husband gets back from parking the car—'

She broke off, her face creasing with pain, and resting her head back she panted through the contraction.

'That's it, nice and easy,' Nick murmured.

The contraction passed, and he folded back the blanket. 'I'm just going to have a look at you, see how long we've got,' he told her, and while Sally opened the obstetrics pack and laid it out, he did a gentle internal to establish the stage of her labour.

'I would say,' he murmured, 'that unless your husband parks that car pretty quickly, he might be out of luck.'

'I'm here,' the man in question said, coming through the curtain in a flurry and skidding to a halt.

'Don't worry, you haven't missed it,' Nick told him with a grin. 'Go and wash your hands. I might give you a job in a minute.'

Good, Sally thought. That means I won't have to be involved. I really, really don't want to be here.

'Do we need the obstetrics squad?' she asked, clutching at straws, but Nick shook his head.

'I don't think so. They have all the fun. Have you had any problems with any of the others, Linda?'

'No, none. They've all been totally straightforward.'

'Right, then, in that case I think we can cope without them. Let me just have a listen. We might call them later to clear up after the excitement's over.'

He put the baby trumpet to Linda's distended abdomen and pressed his ear to the other end, then beckoned to Mr Field. 'Here, have a listen. Lovely and regular.'

Sally met Nick's eyes over the bed and raised a brow hopefully, but he smiled. 'Baby's fine. Call them if you want, but there's no problem. I doubt if they'll get here in time anyway.'

Oh, God, please, let me out of here, Sally thought desperately. Not a baby. Please, not a baby...

'Oh, hell, I want to push,' Mrs Field said through gritted teeth. 'Ow, damn, this is all your fault, Tony.'

'Always is. It's the only time I get any credit for my part in it,' he said with a chuckle, and looked at Nick. 'If the rest were anything to go by, losing her temper means she's about to have it.'

'I think so,' Nick said with a grin, and checked again. 'Yes, the baby's head's crowning. Nice and steady, just pant—that's it, don't push, nice and easy does it.' He put his fingers under the baby's forehead and lifted gently, and the head slipped free, followed in a second by the rest of the baby's body in a slippery rush.

'It's a girl,' he said, lifting up the squalling infant and resting her over Linda's now soft abdomen. 'There you are—clever girl. Well done.'

'Oh, she's gorgeous! Hello, darling,' Linda said, and tears poured down her cheeks. 'Oh, my little one, you're so tiny. Hello, precious. Oh, Tony, look at her!'

Amy was tinier, Sally thought, choking back tears as she watched the ecstatic mother stroke her hand over the precious little body. Tinier and much more frail. This baby was beautiful and healthy and lusty, the way Amy should have been, and a huge sadness welled up in her and threatened to suffocate her.

'Well done,' she murmured, and Linda flashed her a smile, her eyes sparkling with tears.

'Thank you.' She looked back down at the baby, her hand trembling as she touched her, and her husband smiled and blinked back tears and hugged her.

They were so lucky, Sally thought. Four children now, and so much joy. Her heart ached for what she and Nick had lost, and for what they'd never have.

'What are you going to call her?' Nick was asking. Linda didn't hesitate. She just smiled contentedly.

'Amy. It means beloved.'

The pain hit Sally like an express train, shattering her with its intensity, stealing her breath and leaving her devastated.

'I'll get the obstetrics team,' she said, and pushed blindly past Nick into the corridor. She had to get away, to hide.

'Sally?' Ryan called after her as she ran past him, and she hesitated.

'Get the obstetrics team—cubicle ten,' she said, and then kept running until she hit the safety of the Ladies, and then she shut herself in and sank down onto the floor while the pain tore her apart.

*   *   *

'Where's Sally?'

Meg looked up at Nick and shook her head. 'Don't know. Why?'

'Ryan saw her running down the corridor towards the theatre lifts, right after the baby was born, and I haven't seen her since. I don't know where she is, but I want to find her and I don't know where to start. Can you help me? She's not answering her bleep.'

Meg stood up straight away. 'I'll check the loos. That's where she usually goes if something upsets her.'

Nick followed her, fear clutching at him. He'd caught a glimpse of her face as she'd pushed past him, but because of Linda and the baby he'd been unable to follow her.

Now, though, the obstetrics team was there, and he'd left them to it. His first priority had to be Sally, and he was kicking himself for being so blind. Of course the delivery was going to upset her. It was bound to, after what had happened, and to have called the baby Amy was the last straw.

'She's in here,' Meg said, popping her head round the door. 'I can hear her sobbing, but she won't talk to me. Nick, what happened?'

'It's a long story. It's OK, Meg, I'll deal with it. Leave her to me. Is there anyone else in there?'

'No.'

'Right. Keep it that way.'

He pushed past her, knocked on the locked cubicle door and waited, but there was no response, just a hiccuping sob from the other side. He fished a coin out of his pocket and unlocked the door, but he couldn't shift it. She must be sitting against it. He bent down and he could see her hip wedged up against the door.

He shook his head. He had no choice. Going into the adjoining cubicle, he stood on the pan, prayed that the cistern was firmly fixed to the wall, rested his foot on it and peered over.

Sally was hunched up by the door, her head against the wall, and her body was shuddering violently.

Shaking his head, he took a deep breath and hauled himself up, swivelled over the top and dropped down lightly on the floor beside her.

'Sally?' he said softly. 'Sally, talk to me.'

She lifted a face ravaged by tears, and the pain in her eyes tore through him.

'It's all right, sweetheart, I'll get you out of here,' he murmured, and lifted her into his arms.

She hardly weighed anything, he thought as she burrowed up against his chest and wrapped her arms round him like a limpet. He went out into the corridor. Meg was hovering worriedly, and he gave her a grim smile.

'Is she all right?' Meg asked, and he nodded.

'I hope so. Tell Ryan I've taken her home.' He paused in the staffroom, grabbed his jacket and her bag from their lockers and headed for the door, oblivious to the looks he was attracting.

He didn't care. The only thing that mattered to him was getting Sally home and taking care of her. He put her in his car, fastened her seat belt and drove to his house. It didn't even occur to him to take her to her own house; all he knew was that he had to keep her safe, and that meant close by him.

He pulled up outside, unlocked the door and then

led her in on shaky, uncooperative legs. 'Come and sit down,' he instructed, and led her into the sitting room before pushing her gently into a sofa.

She curled up in the foetal position, a cushion clutched to her chest, and he locked his car and ran back inside, almost afraid to leave her.

She hadn't moved. He didn't know what he thought she'd do left alone, just that she needed him, needed something to cling to, something strong and safe and unchangeable, and just then he was the best thing she had.

He sat down beside her, drew her gently into his arms and held her close. 'It's all right, darling,' he murmured. 'It's all right.'

A shudder ran through her, and he ran a hand gently over her hair and smoothed it back, stroking her rhythmically until the shuddering eased and she fell into an uneasy sleep in his arms.

The cat came and miaowed at him, but he ignored it and after a while it went away, presumably to find someone else to feed it, because it came back again about midnight and settled down on the other sofa and snored softly.

Sally's body was relaxed now, exhausted with emotion probably, and Nick eased her out of his arms and went to the loo, made himself a quick sandwich and a drink and came back to the sofa. It might get cold as the night wore on, he thought, and after he'd eaten, he lifted her carefully in his arms without disturbing her and carried her up to his bedroom.

Then, without bothering to undress her or disturb her any more, he laid her down under the quilt, changed into a pair of pyjamas that hadn't seen the light of day in years and slipped in beside her.

She wriggled closer, and he wrapped her in his arms, smoothed her hair gently and then finally, at about three o'clock, he drifted off to sleep.

CHAPTER TEN

SALLY woke to the sound of birds, the purring of a cat and Nick's soft snore in her ear.

She opened her eyes, and found herself face to face with the stray Nick had taken pity on. He seemed to be doing that rather a lot, she thought, remembering yesterday with a shudder of dismay.

She'd made a real fool of herself, but it had just got to her. Silly. One would think by now she'd be over it, but apparently not. Maybe there were some things that you just didn't get over.

Her stomach rumbled, and she realised she hadn't eaten anything since breakfast yesterday. She needed the loo, she needed food and she needed to shower and change before she was due at the hospital in— she peered at Nick's bedside clock—one and a half hours.

She shifted experimentally, and his arm tightened around her waist. He sighed and settled back to sleep, his arm relaxing again, and very carefully, so as not to disturb him, she eased out from under his arm, picked up her shoes from the floor beside the bed and tiptoed down to the kitchen.

The cat was on the stool, miaowing pathetically, and she hunted about and found half a tin of cat food in the fridge. 'You're spoilt. You could go home, you know,' she muttered, and mashed some into a saucer for him.

The cat taken care of, she took a trip to the bathroom, tracked down her handbag in the sitting room and called a taxi, then, after she'd written Nick a note, she let herself out and waited round the corner on the little ring road that ran round the estate.

The taxi came ten minutes later, and once home she showered, pulled on a clean uniform and caught the bus to work. She arrived with five minutes to spare, and used the time to make herself a cup of tea and raid the biscuit tin.

'Not many in there,' the night staff nurse said with a grimace, popping in to get a glass of water. 'It's been one of those nights. We haven't had time to go to the canteen, so we've been stuffing biscuits. We're going to have to put up our contributions to the kitty if it goes on like this. Right, I'll go and finish off. I'll see you for report in a minute.'

'OK. I'll go and get another packet of biscuits on the way,' Sally promised, but she didn't have to because Nick arrived at that moment with three different sorts and tipped them into the biscuit tin.

'Breakfast,' he said economically. 'Since I know you won't have had time for any.'

'You're a star,' she murmured gratefully, and he grunted and sat down across the corner from her and shot her a look.

'You OK?' he said, his voice gruff with concern, and she nodded.

'I'm fine. Thank you for yesterday. It just all got too much.'

'Does anyone here know?'

'About Amy?'

He nodded, and she shook her head. 'No. I didn't

see the need to tell them. I suppose it's going to be pretty difficult to explain otherwise, though, isn't it?'

'Blame it on hormones. Tell them you had PMS.'

She gave a soft laugh. 'I'd almost rather tell them the truth,' she confessed. 'The thought of all that ragging every time I lose it is just too awful to contemplate.'

He smiled at her, but his eyes were worried and she had the distinct feeling he was going to shadow her like a hawk. It was the last thing she needed, but she couldn't say so.

'Nick, I am all right,' she assured him quietly. 'I'm not going to do anything silly, and I won't collapse on you. It just brought it all back, but I'm fine now. It was just—everything.'

'Everything?'

Bad choice of word, she thought, unless she was prepared to explain about her reaction to his affair and how she regretted letting him go, not to mention how very, very much she longed to have his baby.

'Oh, you know, work and so on. I'm tired—you said so yourself. I probably need to take it easy.'

There was a little grunt, as if he didn't quite believe her, but he let it go and concentrated instead on getting the coffee-machine under way.

She drained her tea and stood up, then paused beside him for a moment. 'Thanks for last night, Nick,' she said softly. 'You're a real friend, you know that?'

A shadow flickered in his eyes, and his smile was wry. 'Any time, Sal,' he murmured gruffly. 'Any time.'

*   *   *

It was a long old day, Sally thought. She was calm now, but tired, and all she wanted to do was escape. Still, she had a shift to get through before she could leave, and the day was predictably busy.

'I don't know why we do this job,' she grumbled to Sophie as they cleared up after an ungrateful woman who'd threatened to complain if she didn't get an X-ray.

'It hurts!' the woman had said, but Sally's assurances that she was just bruised had counted for nothing. She'd had to have her X-ray, and Ryan had grumbled about wasting resources and unnecessary exposure to radiation.

'Tell her that,' Sally had said crisply, so Ryan had, and the woman had gone away threatening legal action for verbal abuse.

'What else would you do?' Sophie asked, and an image of little babies sprang instantly to mind.

Stifling it, Sally shrugged. 'I don't know. It's the same everywhere. Most people are really grateful, but there's always one ready to take legal action if you treat them when you have a cold.'

Sophie chuckled, and Sally stripped the paper cloth off the examination couch and replaced it, cobbling the old strip up and putting it in the bin.

'How's your grandmother?' she asked.

'Fine. Mum's found a home. She spent all day looking for one, and yesterday evening we went and had a look, and Gran loved it. She's moving in on the weekend.'

'Wonderful. I hope it works.'

'Oh, it'll be hard at first, I'm sure,' Sophie said philosophically, 'but she knows it's best in the end.'

Meg stuck her head round the door. 'Sally? Someone here to see you—a Mrs Jerome?'

'Mrs Jerome?' Sally said, puzzled, and followed Meg out to the front.

'Over there,' Meg said. 'In the blue dress, with the crutches.'

She'd never seen the woman before, Sally was sure, and yet there was something familiar about that profile.

'Mrs Jerome?' she said, walking up to her. 'I understand you wanted to speak to me.'

The woman turned and smiled tentatively. 'Sister Clarke? Sally? Is that right?'

Sally nodded. 'Yes, that's right. I'm sorry, I don't think I know you.'

'That doesn't surprise me,' the woman said. 'I wasn't looking at my best, I don't suppose. I wanted to thank you for saving my life.'

'Your life?'

'Yes—in the car. I had air leaking from my lung, and you put a needle in and let the air out, and I understand if you hadn't done that I would have died. I just wanted to thank you.'

Sally laughed softly. 'Of course I remember you— I just didn't recognise you, and we didn't have much of a conversation. How are you?'

'Fine. Well, I will be. I've got a few broken ribs and my ankle was broken, but apart from that I'm fine—thanks to you. I just wanted to give you this.'

She handed her an envelope, and Sally shook her head and pushed it back.

'I can't accept money—'

'It's not money. It's an invitation. My husband and

I run a little concert orchestra. It's a pair of complementary tickets to our next performance at Snape Maltings in three weeks. It's nothing, really, just a little thank you—embarrassingly little, compared to what you gave me.'

Touched, Sally took the envelope and gave Mrs Jerome a careful hug. 'Thank you. I'll be sure to come. I'll look forward to it. And you take care, now.'

'I will.'

Mrs Jerome limped out of the door, leaning on her crutches, and smiled up at a man who was obviously waiting for her. He waved at Sally, and she waved back and tucked the envelope into her pocket.

'Did you know her?'

'Yes—I saved her life, just after Nick started when we went out to that pile-up. I didn't recognise her. She gave me tickets for a concert.'

'That's nice.'

'Mmm.' Nick would enjoy it, she thought, and he talked me through the procedure at the accident. Perhaps I'll give them to him. He can take his mistress.

No. It wasn't fair. Mrs Jerome had wanted her to have them, and so she'd go, if necessary alone. Perhaps she'd take Nick, just as a friend.

The phone rang, Ambulance Control giving them advance warning of a seriously injured casualty, and she put the concert tickets out of her mind and concentrated on the job.

It was an RTA victim, a man who hadn't been wearing a seat belt, and he'd been flung against the steering-wheel and had rearranged his face.

'I'll get Tom Kievenaar down,' Nick murmured,

after they'd established a satisfactory airway. 'He's going to need urgent reconstruction.'

There was a great deal of swelling, so it was hard to see how depressed the facial bones were, but the X-rays didn't lie.

'He looks nearly as bad as that girl who jumped off the balcony,' Sally said thoughtfully as they studied the plates with the faciomaxillary surgeon a few minutes later.

'Jodie Farmer? She's doing fine, slowly. Still a bit of a mess, but Plastics will have a go once I've finished messing her about and you'll hardly be able to tell. Her pelvis is more of a problem. She's going to have a permanent limp, I gather.'

'Silly girl.'

'Her boyfriend had just tried to kill her, and then killed himself. She was in quite a mess. She's getting help now, though, and she should be all right. As for our man here, I think a little intervention is going to be in order. OK. Let's get him prepped for Theatre and get him straight up, can we? I'll see what I can do.'

Sally glanced at her watch as she left the hospital. It was four-thirty, only an hour and a half after she was supposed to stop. She called by the flower shop in the main entrance and bought a little posy and a block of florist's foam in a tray, and then retrieved her car from the car park and set off along the country lanes.

It was a lovely afternoon, and after the devastating emotions of yesterday, she felt curiously at peace. Still, she just wanted to touch base…

The car park beside the village hall was deserted

as usual, and she made her way over to the row of tiny graves under the spreading arms of the old yew tree. As she approached, she could see that someone had brought flowers recently to one of the graves, and then suddenly, her steps slowed.

They were on Amy's grave.

She walked slowly up to it and looked down, her eyes filling. They were beautiful flowers, not huge, ornate lilies but little dainty things, baby's breath and freesias and tiny rosebuds in soft yellow and creamy white—the same colours she'd chosen to bring with her that afternoon.

Sally knelt down on the grass a little abruptly, and stared at them.

Nick.

He'd brought his daughter flowers, the only thing he could do for her. The tears clumped on her lashes and spilled over, and she brushed them away.

There was no message tucked in amongst the blossoms. Nick wouldn't be given to sentimental outpourings or public displays of emotion. Instead, he would have come here alone and placed them solemnly on her grave in a private moment of farewell.

Oh, Nick, she thought, I'm so sorry.

Her hand reached out to touch the petals, and she focused on them with effort. Some of the flowers were a little tired now, so she eased them out and replaced them with the ones from her posy, squeezing the rest in around the edges, then sat back on her heels and stared at them sightlessly, deep in thought.

If Nick had brought flowers to Amy, then maybe that had been why he'd asked about a florist? Maybe he didn't have a mistress. In fact, it seemed unlikely, really, unless he'd ordered the flowers for Amy as an afterthought while he'd been ordering the others, but she didn't think he'd do that.

Not the first time, at least.

In which case…

'I need to talk to your daddy, my darling,' she said to Amy. 'Wish me luck.'

She blew a kiss to the little headstone, scrambled to her feet and ran back to the car, her heart pounding, impatience clawing at her.

She drove back to Nick's house, drumming her fingers on the steering-wheel as she sat in the rush-hour traffic, but then finally she was there, parking the car down the side of the garden by his fence.

His car was on the drive, to her relief, and screwing up her courage she hurried to the front door and rang the bell, her heart in her mouth. Her palms were damp, and she scrubbed them against the sides of her dress while she waited. He must be there. He must have heard her.

A shadow moved and the door swung open. He smiled a little cautiously. 'Hi,' he offered. 'Are you OK?'

'I don't know. Maybe. Can I come in?'

'Of course.' He stepped back, and closed the door behind her. 'Tea?'

'Not now. Can we go into your study?'

'Sure.' He led the way up the spiral staircase to the lovely leafy room, and she absently noticed her little bonsai tree in pride of place on his shelves. It looked well. Oh, Lord, where to start—

'Sally?'

Her eyes snapped to his face, then away again, then

back, holding this time, hanging on for dear life to the steady blue flame of his eyes.

'You took flowers to Amy,' she said abruptly.

His face grew wary. 'Yes. I'm sorry—I should have asked.'

'Asked?' she said, astonished.

'Yes, asked—if you minded. I never meant to upset you. I'm sorry. I didn't think about it.'

'Why should I mind?' she asked, genuinely puzzled. 'She was your daughter, Nick. Of course I don't mind. You have every right to take her flowers as often as you like.'

'I don't think so,' he said softly, sadly. 'I let you go. I didn't keep in touch, I didn't get back to you when you phoned. I lost the right to call her my daughter.'

'No!' Sally said firmly. 'Oh, no. No, you didn't. It was my fault. I should never have let you get out of touch. I knew where you were, I managed to track you down, I should have persisted. I should have told you when I knew I was pregnant, instead of keeping it a secret, and then you would have seen her, and held her…'

Tears of regret splashed down her cheeks, but she ignored them. 'I'm so sorry, Nick. I kept her away from you, and I shouldn't have done, and I'm so, so sorry. If I could turn back the clock—'

She broke off, and he stared at her, motionless, for a moment.

'What?' he asked in a strangled voice. 'What would you do?'

She lifted her chin defiantly. 'I would never have let you go. I wouldn't have moved with you, at least not at first, but I would never have let you walk out of my life like that. I loved you too much to lose you.'

She took a steadying breath, and carried on. 'I love you too much now to let you go without a fight.'

'No fight,' he murmured, shaking his head slowly from side to side. 'I spent the last two years or so looking for you intermittently, in between bouts of common sense. I'm not going to lose you now I've found you.'

'Oh, Nick,' she whispered raggedly, and then she was in his arms, and he was kissing her as if he'd die without her. Her arms slid round him, her hands tracing the powerful column of his spine, and he groaned and lifted his head and looked down at her, his eyes on fire.

'I want to make love to you,' he said gently.

'Well, don't let me stop you,' she said with a weak attempt at humour, and he smiled and took her by the hand and led her down the spiral staircase and up the other one to his bedroom.

There he turned her into his arms and kissed her tenderly again, brushing the hair back off her face and trailing hot, moist kisses over her jaw and down the soft column of her throat.

She stopped him with his hands on the fastening of her uniform dress, and he looked up to her eyes and paused. 'What?' he murmured.

'Are you having an affair?' she asked nervously.

He laughed, a wry, choked little laugh without humour. 'An affair. You really think I'd be doing this to you if I was having an affair?'

She shook her head. 'No. Well, at least, I hoped not, but…'

'What?'

'Ryan said you were asking about flowers.'

'Flowers?' he echoed, and then his face cleared. 'For Amy,' he reminded her. 'Only for Amy. There's only one woman in the world I want to be having an affair with, and she keeps stalling.' His mouth was smiling, but the smile didn't reach his eyes.

The tension went out of her, together with the last shred of doubt. She reached up her hand and cradled his jaw, relishing the slight roughness of the stubble against her trembling palm. 'That's all right, then,' she said with a slow smile, 'because I've stopped stalling now.'

'Thank goodness for that,' he said, and he claimed her lips again.

Sally lay sprawled across Nick, her fingers idly tracing the light scatter of hair on his chest as she listened to his heartbeat. One leg was wedged between his, her toes snuggled against his calf, and she could feel one hand stroking her lightly, feathering caresses down her spine.

'Did I imagine it, or did you say you'd been looking for me?' she said, and his hand stilled.

'No, you didn't imagine it.'

She propped herself up on one elbow and looked down at him. 'So how come, then?'

He shrugged. 'I couldn't get you out of my mind. Every time I tried to have a relationship, it failed. After a while I realised that it was because they weren't you.'

'Sounds as if you were busy,' she said, stifling a pang of jealousy. Of course he'd had affairs! He was young and healthy—

His soft laugh cut off her train of thought. 'Hardly. Most of them fell at the first hurdle and we didn't get past the initial date, but there was one—I told you about her. Marilyn. It seemed to be working for a while. We were reasonably happy. Then she started dropping hints, and her mother kept making little noises about wedding bells, and I just realised suddenly that I didn't love her. I was fond of her, she was a lovely girl, but I wasn't in love with her.'

'So you ended it.'

'So I ended it,' he agreed, 'and I spent a few weeks trying to track you down, but it was four years since I'd heard from you, and the trail was well and truly cold. Not that I expected anything else, because I'd failed to find you four days after you called, never mind four years, but I tried, anyway. First I tried all the hospitals—do you have any idea how many hospitals there are in the country, and how many Sally Clarkes there are, and how incredibly cagey everyone is about revealing information about staff?'

'I'm sorry,' she murmured, and kissed him.

'Mmm. I can stand a lot of that.'

'Not till you've told me how you found me.'

'Oh, that. I gave up. I tried phone books. There are probably four million S. Clarkes listed, but none of them were you.'

'Three years ago? I was living with my mother and stepfather.'

'Ah. Right. And two years ago, and last year?'

She smiled apologetically. 'I lived in the nurses'

accommodation for a while, and then I had a flat and a mobile phone. I only got a land line and went in the phone book about six months ago, after I bought the house.'

'By which time I'd found you,' he said.

She sat up straighter and stared down at him. 'You found me six months ago?'

He nodded. 'Oh, yes. Someone came to Peterborough from here, and they were talking one day after one of the nurses let rip about something, and he said you think that's bad, you haven't seen Sally Clarke's temper!' His smile was wry. 'That struck a chord,' he said drily, 'so I asked a few questions, and it sounded like you—right age, right physical description—'

'Right temperament?'

He grinned. 'You do have a wicked temper, my darling,' he teased gently, and she snuggled down into the crook of his arm and smiled to herself.

'Go on. I want to know how you wangled the job.'

'It was advertised. It was sheer coincidence. I applied for it, got the job, and came for interview. You were here.'

'You saw me?' she said, jackknifing upright again and twisting to look down at him indignantly. 'You saw me and you didn't say anything?'

He shook his head. 'I couldn't. I was being towed down the corridor by Ryan, and, anyway, I was so stunned I don't think I could have spoken to you. Ryan was talking to me, telling me about the department, and I didn't hear a word. I was just poleaxed.'

'How do you think I felt when I saw you the first

time the other week?' she asked. 'You could have
warned me.'

He reached up a hand and touched her face. 'I'm
sorry, Sal. I didn't want to warn you. I wanted to see
your face, to read your reactions so I knew how to
play it.'

'And?'

His smile was wry. 'And I thought you were still
angry with me. I wondered if moving here had all
been a dreadful mistake, but I was locked into the
contract and I still had a few weeks to consider the
consultancy—'

'What consultancy?' she squeaked, kneeling up beside him and glaring at him. 'You haven't mentioned
a consultancy!'

'That's because it's still hush-hush, and they
haven't advertised yet. They're expanding the department. They've got another consultancy post coming up in January. Ryan wants me to have it. I said
I'd give him my answer in a few days.'

She sat back down on her heels abruptly. 'And?'
she asked, fear gnawing at her again. 'What will you
say?'

'That depends on you,' he told her, his eyes serious
now. 'I don't know if you want me to take it, or if
you want more time to think about us...'

'What about us?' she asked warily.

'About whether or not you want to marry me,' he
said quietly.

She felt the fear ease, and smiled. 'Why don't you
ask me?' she suggested.

He pulled a wry face. 'Because I'm afraid you'll
say no?'

'Not in this lifetime,' she assured him, and with a groan of relief he drew her down into his arms and kissed her hungrily.

'Uh-uh,' she said, wriggling out of the way. 'Ask me, please! You have to do it properly.'

'On one knee?'

She shook her head. 'That would mean letting go of you.'

'OK.' He smiled down at her, then his eyes grew serious. 'I love you, Sally,' he said softly. 'I know we screwed up before, but I won't let it happen again. Marry me—please? Have my babies? Let's be a family. I've missed you so much. I don't think I could bear it—'

'Yes,' she said, and, wrapping her arms around his neck, she drew him down for a kiss. 'Yes,' she said again after a long, mind-drugging minute. 'Oh, yes…'

Modern Romance™
...seduction and
passion guaranteed

Tender Romance™
...love affairs that
last a lifetime

Sensual Romance™
...sassy, sexy and
seductive

Sizzling Romance™
...sultry days and
steamy nights

Medical Romance™
...medical drama on
the pulse

Historical Romance™
...rich, vivid and
passionate

29 new titles every month.

*With all kinds of Romance for
every kind of mood...*

MILLS & BOON®

Makes any time special™

MAT3

Coming Home

Scandal drove David away
Now love will draw him home . . .

PENNY JORDAN

FREE

4 BOOKS
AND A SURPRISE GIFT!

We would like to take this opportunity to thank you for reading this Mills & Boon® book by offering you the chance to take FOUR more specially selected titles from the Medical Romance™ series absolutely FREE! We're also making this offer to introduce you to the benefits of the Reader Service™—

★ FREE home delivery   ★ FREE gifts and competitions
★ FREE monthly Newsletter   ★ Exclusive Reader Service discounts
       ★ Books available before they're in the shops

Accepting these FREE books and gift places you under no obligation to buy; you may cancel at any time, even after receiving your free shipment. Simply complete your details below and return the entire page to the address below. **You don't even need a stamp!**

YES! Please send me 4 free Medical Romance books and a surprise gift. I understand that unless you hear from me, I will receive 6 superb new titles every month for just £2.49 each, postage and packing free. I am under no obligation to purchase any books and may cancel my subscription at any time. The free books and gift will be mine to keep in any case.

M1ZEC

Ms/Mrs/Miss/Mr ....Initials ....
BLOCK CAPITALS PLEASE

Surname ....

Address ....

....

....Postcode ....

Send this whole page to:
UK: FREEPOST CN81, Croydon, CR9 3WZ
EIRE: PO Box 4546, Kilcock, County Kildare (stamp required)